Murder in the Maze

LOTTIE SPRIGG COUNTRY HOUSE MYSTERY BOOK 3

MARTHA BOND

Lottie Sprigg Country House Mystery Series

* * *

'WHAT'S THIS?' said Lord Buckley-Phipps. 'The post has only just arrived, Duxbury?'

It was mid-morning in the sitting room at Fortescue Manor.

'I'm afraid so, my lord.' The butler began to hand out the envelopes.

'But it's almost eleven o'clock. It should have been here at breakfast!'

'The postal service is awfully unreliable these days,' said Lady Buckley-Phipps.

'These letters could contain important matters,' added her husband. 'One shouldn't have to wait until coffee time to receive them. Perhaps you could have a word with the postman, Duxbury?'

'I will do, my lord.'

The butler handed the final envelope in his hand to Lottie. It was a small, square envelope with the address carefully written in blue ink.

'You've received some post, Lottie?' said her employer,

1

Mrs Moore. Her lap was filled with a pile of letters forwarded from her London home.

'Yes.'

Lottie's hands trembled. She felt sure this letter was a reply from a lady she had written to.

Lord Buckley-Phipps continued to grumble about the postal service as he slit open envelopes with a sharp letter opener.

'Oh wonderful!' said Lady Buckley-Phipps. 'My London seamstress informs me she has received the fabrics from Paris for my summer wardrobe. About time too!'

Lottie stared at the little envelope in her hand.

Was this a letter from her mother?

She glanced down at Rosie, her Welsh Pembroke Corgi, who sat by her feet. Rosie's large brown eyes looked back at her, and Lottie patted her on the head. With Rosie's silent encouragement, Lottie put her thumbnail under the fold of the envelope and began to open it.

Lottie had grown up in Oswestry Orphanage and had never known her parents. Recently, she had learned from the orphanage that a lady had visited and asked about her. She had also learned the lady was a regular visitor to the local library, and Lottie believed she had seen her there once. She had heard the lady's companion at the time call her Josephine.

Since then, Lottie had found four local women called Josephine, and she had written to them asking if they were the lady who had enquired about her at the orphanage. Two had replied to say they weren't and Lottie had heard nothing from the other two.

Until now.

Lottie peeled open the last bit of the envelope and pulled out the folded letter. The paper felt thin and cheap.

'Who's your letter from, Lottie?' asked Mrs Moore.

'Just a friend from the orphanage, I think.' She didn't

want to say anything more in front of everyone else. And if the letter was from her mother, how was she going to contain her emotion?

Mrs Moore returned to her own letters and Lottie carefully opened the little square of paper.

Chapter Two

THE LETTER from Josephine Brambling was short:

Dear Miss Sprigg,
Thank you for your letter, I apologise for my late reply. I was visiting my sister in the Midlands.
I'm not the lady who was asking after you in the orphanage. I'm sorry if you were hoping for good news.
I wish you luck in finding her.
Yours sincerely,
Mrs Josephine Brambling

Lottie sighed and re-folded the paper. It was another disappointment.

But she could look for another Josephine. Her search wasn't over yet. She patted Rosie on the head and tried to swallow the lump in her throat.

'Golly,' said Mrs Moore, brandishing a large card with gilded edges. 'An invitation from Lord and Lady Chichester!'

'An invitation to what?' said Lady Buckley-Phipps. Her tone suggested she was annoyed she hadn't received one.

'A weekend party to celebrate their first wedding anniversary. Has it really been a year already? It doesn't seem that long ago when the newspapers were filled with nothing but news of Lord Chichester's divorce.'

'Very scandalous it was indeed,' said Lady Buckley-Phipps.

'I don't remember it,' said Lottie.

'You probably weren't very interested in it, that's why, Lottie,' said Mrs Moore. 'It made headlines because Lord and Lady Chichester were from two distinguished aristocratic families. They were married for many years and had five children together. Then she petitioned for divorce when he had an affair with a West End starlet.'

Lady Buckley-Phipps rolled her eyes. 'Isn't it always the way?'

'Always the way?' said Lord Buckley-Phipps. 'What do you mean by that, Lucinda?'

'These lords with loyal wives and a happy family get charmed by some young actress and they can't help themselves.'

'You make it sound as if we're all at it!' said her husband.

'I know you're not, Ivan. But it's becoming a common theme these days.'

'Having been married three times myself, I'm hardly the sort who may comment on other people's marriages,' said Mrs Moore. 'However, no sooner had the Chichester divorce been settled, than Lord Chichester swiftly married the West End starlet. Her name was Ruby Higgins, famous for being in the Pom-Pom Duo.'

'I think I've heard of them,' said Lottie.

'The Pom-Pom Duo,' scoffed Lady Buckley-Phipps. 'Terribly tacky.'

'But they were very popular, Lucinda,' said Mrs Moore.

'And still are, although I don't think the second Lady Chichester performs as much as she used to.'

'I'm surprised Lord Chichester allows his wife to parade around on a stage waving pom-poms about,' said Lord Buckley-Phipps. 'It's not respectable for a lady who's married into the aristocracy.'

'I expect she won't be told,' said his wife. 'She's probably one of these modern young women who is intent on doing whatever they like. Have you seen the Pom-Pom Duo perform, Roberta?'

'I saw them in a show at the Gaiety Theatre a couple of years ago. The show was held to raise money for a children's hospital and it had a variety of acts. It wasn't my choice to see the Pom-Pom Duo, they just appeared on the stage and did their thing.'

'Which is what?' asked Lord Buckley-Phipps.

'Well, there was pom-pom waving, which you've already mentioned, Ivan. And singing and dancing too. They're actually quite a talented pair of girls.'

'And now one of them is Lady Chichester of Hamilton Hall,' said Lady Buckley-Phipps. 'There must be quite an age gap between her and her husband.'

'Yes, I believe it's almost thirty years,' said Mrs Moore.

'I think it's quite obvious she only married him for his money and status. It's every chorus girl's dream, isn't it? To be of lowly birth and become lady of the manor.'

'Perhaps you've got it all wrong, Lucinda,' said Lord Buckley-Phipps. 'Maybe they genuinely love one another. I know it doesn't look good that the old chap had an affair with her while married. But she's now his wife and maybe that's down to good old-fashioned love.'

'Perhaps so, Ivan,' said his wife. 'But I doubt it. Anyway, when is the party, Roberta?'

'The weekend after next. I'm looking forward to a trip to Buckinghamshire. It will be exciting, won't it, Lottie?'

Chapter Three

'A WEEKEND PARTY AT HAMILTON HALL,' said Mrs Moore. 'I can't wait!' She, Lottie and Rosie were taking a leisurely walk around the lake in the sunny grounds of Fortescue Manor. It was springtime and birds fluttered and sang in the fresh green foliage on the trees.

Rosie ambled by the water's edge, sniffing interesting smells and watching the ducks who were keeping a safe distance from her.

'Have you visited Hamilton Hall before?' Lottie asked her employer.

'Yes. Although that was when Lord Chichester was married to the first Lady Chichester. I spent a very pleasant weekend with them and we had some fun games of croquet. I first met the Chichesters at a party hosted by a Syrian prince at the Savoy Hotel just after the war. Lord Chichester is a charming gentleman, despite his slip-up with the starlet. The first Lady Chichester is delightful too. I believe she now calls herself Lady Forbes-Chichester to distinguish herself from the second Lady Chichester. Forbes was her maiden name. And Hamilton Hall is simply beautiful. Apparently, it was quite rundown when Lord Chichester inherited it. It's famous for its maze.'

'A maze? I like the sound of that.'

'Apparently, the maze is quite ancient. It had fallen into ruin by the time the present Lord Chichester took over the estate. He restored the maze and extended it too. I've heard it's the largest maze in England, but that could just be a rumour.'

'Have you met the second Lady Chichester?'

'No. I've only ever seen her on stage and that was before she married Lord Chichester. I missed their wedding because it took place while we were in Venice last year. I've heard she's perfectly pleasant, but she'll be quite different from the first Lady Chichester, that's for sure. Anyway, we must begin making plans! I think we need to return to London at the end of this week. It will be nice to see the house in Chelsea again and we'll have some time to do some clothes shopping too. What do you say, Lottie?'

Lottie had no desire to go to London, she liked Fortescue Manor too much. She had worked there as a maid before Mrs Moore had employed her and it felt like home to her. And how could she continue her search for her mother if she was going away?

But Lottie couldn't argue. She was employed to accompany Mrs Moore wherever she went.

'I think it's a good idea,' she said with a smile.

'Wonderful! And Rosie will see London for the first time. We're all going to have a lovely time.'

Chapter Four

'I'M SO sad you're going away,' said Mildred the maid as Lottie fastened her suitcase.

'Me too,' said Lottie. 'But I promise to write.'

'Good. So do I.' They gave each other a quick embrace and Rosie squeezed between their legs so she could be included too.

Lottie then took one last look around her bedroom. It was a small, simple room which had belonged to her when she'd been a maid.

'You can borrow my books whenever you like, Mildred.' She pointed at the shelf above her bed.

'Oh, you know I don't read very much.'

'You will once you start one of those books. They're detective stories!'

'I'll give them a try, I suppose.'

'And if a letter arrives for me while I'm away, please could you forward it on to Mrs Moore's Chelsea address?'

'Yes. Are you expecting something?'

'A letter from the final Josephine. If she wants to write to me, that is.'

'She should do.'

'She might not. Perhaps the lady who asked about me at the orphanage has changed her mind about seeing me.'

'I don't see why she would do that.'

'Or perhaps she can't bring herself to reply to the letter. Maybe she's too nervous.'

'I suppose that could be possible. But if she's too nervous to reply to your letter, then why did she ask after you at the orphanage?'

'I don't know. I'm just trying to think of reasons why the fourth Josephine hasn't replied yet.'

'Perhaps she's away. The third Josephine was away for a bit, wasn't she? The fourth one might be too. Or perhaps she hasn't received your letter for some reason.'

'Oh no, I hope that's not the case. Maybe I could try writing to her again. But if she doesn't want to hear from me, then that would annoy her, I imagine.'

'I promise I'll forward any letter which arrives for you, Lottie,' said Mildred. 'I think you should try to enjoy your travels and try not to worry about the fourth Josephine too much.'

'Yes. That's a good suggestion. I can think about what to do next when we return. It's difficult to do anything about it when I'm in London and Buckinghamshire.'

Mildred checked her watch. 'Your taxi was due to arrive five minutes ago, Lottie! You'd better get downstairs!'

'Goodness!' Lottie picked up her case and dashed out of her room, with Rosie and Mildred following. 'Fortunately, it will take about ten minutes to get all of Mrs Moore's luggage in the taxi,' said Lottie, as they dashed down the stairs.

* * *

The train arrived at London Euston railway station at teatime and, half an hour later, Lottie, Rosie and Mrs Moore were getting out of the taxi outside the house in Chelsea.

'Isn't it good to be back, Lottie?' said Mrs Moore as their luggage was carried into the house. She stood by the railings of her grand four-storey townhouse. 'Just breathe in that London air!' She gave a cough. 'Actually, don't. I'd forgotten how smoky it is here, even on a lovely spring day.'

Mrs Mitchell, the housekeeper, was a rosy-cheeked, grey-haired lady who gave them a warm welcome. She'd kept the house clean and tidy and took pride in showing them the new table linens and curtains she'd recently purchased for the home.

Rosie adjusted to London life quickly. She enjoyed sniffing the myriad of smells on the busy streets and happily made friends with a variety of local dogs. The riverside Botanic Gardens were close to Mrs Moore's home and Lottie found lots of new walks for her and Rosie to take.

Mrs Moore took Lottie to her favourite dress shops on King's Road and it wasn't long before Lottie had a range of new outfits for the summer. Her favourite was the evening dress for the party at Hamilton Hall. It was long and elegant and made of lemon-coloured silk. Mrs Moore also bought her silk evening gloves, a feather boa and a jewelled headband. When Lottie tried the outfit on in the shop, she barely recognised herself.

Mrs Moore chose an evening gown of plum-purple satin. It had a fitted bodice and a voluminous skirt. Mrs Moore preferred eye-catching outfits over anything fashionable.

Soon the day arrived when it was time to travel to Buckinghamshire. The hour-long train journey took them north-west of London to a pleasant little railway station called Cheddington. There, a chauffeur with a smart motorcar met them.

'Lord and Lady Chichester are keenly awaiting your arrival,' he said.

'Marvellous!' Mrs Moore clapped her hands with glee. 'We can't wait to see them too!'

HAMILTON HALL WAS A SPRAWLING red brick building with mullioned windows, tall chimneys and steeply pitched roofs. Its formal gardens were filled with geometric flowerbeds, topiary and statues.

The gravelled driveway crunched beneath the car as the chauffeur drove Lottie, Rosie and Mrs Moore to the grand entrance of the house.

'This place is just as beautiful as I remembered,' said Mrs Moore as she examined it through her lorgnette.

Two footmen showed them to the door where a sombre-faced butler met them in a high-ceilinged entrance hall. The marble floor was tiled black and white like a chessboard. Decorative pilasters lined the walls and Lottie's gaze was drawn to the colourful fresco on the ceiling where classical-looking figures cavorted in flowing robes. Paintings in heavy gold frames hung between the pilasters and one painting was twice the size of all the others. It was a painting of a young woman in a fashionable, flame-red dress standing beneath a tree in a serene landscape. Lottie guessed she was the second Lady

Chichester. She had a pale heart-shaped face, short brown wavy hair, and a sultry expression.

'Golly, what a striking portrait,' said Mrs Moore. 'It feels like her eyes are following us, doesn't it?'

Their footsteps echoed on the floor as they passed Lady Chichester's watchful gaze and followed the butler to a doorway near the foot of a grand staircase. They were shown into a peach and gold drawing room with plush furnishings and tall windows overlooking the garden. Lottie now saw the lady from the portrait in real life as she took a step towards them with her husband.

Lord Chichester was a stocky, wide-bellied man with a pointed grey beard and twinkling blue eyes. 'How delightful it is to see you again, Mrs Moore,' he said.

'And you too, Lord Chichester. Thank you so much for the invitation to your lovely home and I wish you and your wife a happy wedding anniversary.'

'Talking of which, here she is!' Lady Chichester stepped forward, looking cheerier than she did in her portrait. 'Ruby, meet Mrs Roberta Moore, a dear friend of mine.'

'How lovely to meet you,' she said.

Mrs Moore introduced Lottie, then the Chichesters both admired Rosie and gave her some pats.

'Although I haven't met you in person before, Lady Chichester, I saw you perform at the Gaiety a couple of years ago,' said Mrs Moore.

'Oh, did you?' Lady Chichester grew bashful. 'I hope you enjoyed the performance.'

'I very much did.'

'Miss Darby, my partner in the Pom-Pom Duo, is here.' She beckoned to a blonde lady who was reclining in a chair by a window. 'Come and meet Mrs Moore and Miss Sprigg, Daisy!'

Daisy Darby got to her feet, smoothed her fashionable

long jacket and stepped over to meet them. She didn't smile very much, and Lottie wondered if she was a reluctant guest.

They exchanged greetings, then Lady Chichester said, 'You'll meet our manager, Quentin Lawrence, later. He and his wife are just freshening up in their room.'

'Quentin Lawrence the famous songwriter?' said Mrs Moore.

'Yes. He's a man of many talents. Perhaps you've met his wife, Maria? She's a Shakespearean actress.'

'Yes, I believe I have met her once or twice.'

'You'll see them at dinner,' said Lord Chichester. 'We're hosting just a few guests for dinner this evening and then a cohort of guests will descend on us for dancing and a few surprise performances too.'

'Wonderful! I can't wait, Lord Chichester,' said Mrs Moore. 'And I must say that I quite admire your portrait in the entrance hall, Lady Chichester.'

'Oh, that old thing!' She grew bashful again.

'It's a good size, isn't it?' said Lord Chichester. 'And the paint on it has only just dried! We got it hung up last week. I commissioned one of my favourite artists to paint it as a gift for Ruby on our first wedding anniversary.'

'Well he's certainly a talented artist.'

'Yes, he's painted me and my family over the years and I thought it was about time that Ruby had a portrait all of her own.'

'I got terribly bored sitting for it,' said Lady Chichester. 'But I think he captured a good likeness, even if it is a little too flattering.'

'You look quite beautiful in it, Lady Chichester,' said Mrs Moore. 'How I wish someone had painted me while I was still in my prime. You need to make the most of it while you can.'

Daisy Darby chuckled, and Lady Chichester's smile faded a little.

Chapter Six

A MAID SHOWED Mrs Moore and Lottie to their rooms. Mrs Moore's room was pink and rose-themed. It had a balcony and overlooked the gardens.

'There's the famous maze!' said Mrs Moore as she opened the door to the balcony. Lottie looked out and saw the expansive labyrinth of neatly clipped hedges.

'Goodness,' she said. 'It's huge! How does anyone find their way in and out?'

'It takes a while, but you get there in the end. I lived to tell the tale!'

Lottie's room was smaller but comfortably furnished in pastel green.

'I'm sorry I haven't found time yet to put your clothes in your wardrobe, madam,' said the maid. 'I'll do it now.' She looked about Lottie's age and was sandy-haired with green eyes.

'Oh, don't be sorry at all,' said Lottie. 'And there's no need, I can do it myself. To be honest with you, I would find it quite awkward if you put my clothes away for me. I used to work as a maid, you see.'

'You did?'

'Yes. Before I became a travelling companion to Mrs Moore.'

The maid smiled. 'So you know what it's like.'

'Absolutely. And I'm guessing you didn't find the time to put my clothes away because you were busy with all of Mrs Moore's things. She doesn't travel lightly.'

The maid grinned. 'She has lots of lovely things, though. Do you enjoy being a travelling companion?'

'Yes, I've visited some lovely places which I never imagined I'd see.'

'I like the idea of that.'

Rosie sniffed at the maid's skirt, then rested against her leg. She patted the corgi on the head. 'I hope you and your dog enjoy your stay here, Miss Sprigg.'

'Thank you, we will. Do you mind me asking your name?'

'Sally. Just let me know if you need anything.'

'I will do! Thank you, Sally.'

Chapter Seven

LOTTIE DRESSED for dinner and put on the lemon silk dress. When she added the silk gloves, feather boa and beaded headband, she felt over-dressed.

'I don't really look like me, do I, Rosie?' she said as she looked at herself in the mirror. But then she heard the dinner gong and knew she had no longer to dwell on it.

At dinner, they met Mr and Mrs Lawrence. Quentin Lawrence was a lean-faced man with prominent cheekbones and oiled hair. He spoke with his chin raised and his nose sticking in the air.

Spring vegetable soup was served and Lottie worried she might accidentally drip some onto her evening gown.

'Which song of yours is most popular, Mr Lawrence?' asked Mrs Moore. She was resplendent in a swathe of plum-purple satin.

'*Five Old Ladies In The Ritz*,' he replied. 'Although many people tell me how much they enjoy *No Sugar In My Tea, I'm Sweet Enough*.'

'That's a good one too,' said Mrs Moore. 'Many of your

songs are quite famous, aren't they? I didn't realise how many of them I know.'

'Well, I've been at it a fair few years now, so it's probably not surprising.'

'You deserve some time off, Quentin,' said his wife, Maria. She was a stern-faced lady with dark raven hair and a sharp nose.

'You can't take time off in this business,' said Quentin. 'There's always someone trying to get ahead of you. If you take a break, then you may as well be forgotten about.'

'Oh dear,' said Mrs Moore. 'That sounds quite cut-throat.'

'Quentin's right,' said Maria. 'And it's the same in the world of acting.'

'It's all just so competitive,' said Lady Chichester.

Daisy Darby gave a sad nod in agreement.

'Do you only act in Shakespearean roles, Mrs Lawrence?' asked Mrs Moore.

'That's right.'

'You've done nearly all of them, haven't you, darling?' said her husband.

'Yes.' Mrs Lawrence counted them off on her fingers. She wore large sparkling rings over her evening gloves. 'Desdemona, Ophelia, Hermia, Titania, Rosalind, Juliet...'

'When were you Juliet?' asked her husband.

'Early in my career. For many years I was able to pass as much younger, you know. Now where was I? Oh yes, Viola. That's another one.'

'There's one role which has eluded you, hasn't it, darling?' said her husband.

'Thank you for pointing that out.' She took a sip of soup.

'Which role is that?' asked Mrs Moore.

'Lady Macbeth,' said Mr Lawrence. 'The best role in the Scottish play.'

'You've never played Lady Macbeth?' asked Mrs Moore.

'No. Quite ridiculous, really, because I know all the lines.'

'You regularly recite them at home, don't you, darling?'

'That's because I've been rehearsing for this evening.'

'Are we going to be treated to a performance?' asked Mrs Moore.

'You shall have to wait and see.'

'That probably means yes,' said a lady with maroon hair. Her name was Margaret Stanley-Piggot and her late husband had been an old friend of Lord Chichester's. She wore a sapphire blue dress with matching gloves and lots of sparkling jewellery. Lord Chichester had told them earlier that she was one of the richest widows in the country. 'There's a production of Macbeth at the Princess Theatre in the West End at the moment,' she continued. 'Did you not go for the role, Mrs Lawrence?'

'We always refer to it as the Scottish play. We never name it!'

'Whoops. I think I've heard that before. Isn't it bad luck or something?'

'Very bad luck. And yes, I know of the production, but I didn't go for the role because I'm not keen on that particular director.'

'Well, he's done a good job of it, there have been some glowing reviews.'

'Have there? I wouldn't know.' Mrs Lawrence gave a sniff and looked a little wounded.

'Are you ever tempted to perform any of your husband's songs, Mrs Lawrence?' asked Mrs Moore.

'No. I don't perform to the music hall crowds as a rule.'

'Music hall?' said Lady Chichester. 'It's a little more than that!'

'Alright then, popular entertainment or whatever you like to call it. I'm afraid it attracts quite a bit of riff-raff. I prefer performing Shakespeare because it attracts a more discerning audience.'

'But where there's riff-raff, there's money to be made,' said Quentin Lawrence. 'Lady Chichester and Miss Darby would agree with me, would they not?'

The two ladies nodded.

'I would like to write sophisticated pieces, but if I want to stay at work, then I must write what's popular,' he said. 'It's the way of the world these days.'

'Yes it is,' said Mrs Stanley-Piggot. 'Although I agree with your wife, Mr Lawrence. A good bit of Shakespeare is more entertaining. Especially the tragedies. There's nothing like a good tragedy to entertain oneself of an evening.'

'I agree!' said Mrs Lawrence. 'I enjoy exploring the darker side of human nature.'

'Do you indeed?' said Mrs Moore.

'Yes. I would encourage you to see a play with deep meaning to it, Mrs Moore. It can make you question life and your existence.'

'Can it? If I'm honest, I think I prefer listening to *Five Old Ladies In The Ritz.*'

'Hear, hear!' said Mr Lawrence. 'What do you say, Lord Chichester?'

'Oh, I refuse to say. I'm remaining firmly on the fence with this one. I don't want to get into trouble with any of my guests. Or my wife, for that matter!'

Lady Chichester smiled and fluttered her eyelashes.

'Well, let's change the subject then,' said Mrs Stanley-Piggot. 'You'll never guess what I bought yesterday.'

'What did you buy, Margaret?' asked Lord Chichester.

'Nelson's Column.'

Chapter Eight

THERE WAS silence around the dinner table for a moment.

'Nelson's Column?' said Lord Chichester. 'The two-hundred-foot column in the middle of Trafalgar Square?'

'It's one hundred and sixty-nine feet, actually,' said Mrs Stanley-Piggot. 'That's what it says in the paperwork.'

'It's possible to own it, is it?'

'Yes, of course it is. Everything has its price, you know.'

'Who sold it to you?'

'An extremely nice broker. Mr Jones was his name. And he was extremely helpful in negotiating a good deal for me. Ever since Francis died, I've spent a great deal of time thinking about what to do with all the money he left. And this seems like such a good investment. After all, Nelson's Column is a monument which we can all treasure and enjoy, isn't it?'

'Well, I never,' said Lord Chichester. 'I didn't realise you could just buy these things.'

'I can put you in touch with Mr Jones if you like, William. He's extremely good at these things. He might tell you about other landmarks which are available for sale.'

'Does the sale include the lions at the base of the column?' asked Mrs Lawrence.

'Yes, I think they must be included,' said Mrs Stanley-Piggot. 'They're all part of the same feature, surely?'

'It sounds like you need to check that, Margaret,' said Lord Chichester. 'You probably need to make sure that Nelson himself at the top is also included.'

'He must be! I paid enough money for it.'

'How much did you pay?'

She lowered her voice a little. 'It is a large sum of money, I'm afraid.'

'How much?'

'Twenty thousand pounds.'

Everyone gasped. And another silence fell.

'I'm sorry to be the bearer of bad news,' said Miss Darby. 'But you've been had.'

'I beg your pardon?'

'You've been fooled, Mrs Stanley-Piggot. This Mr Jones, or whoever he is, is a confidence trickster.'

'He absolutely is not! He has a proper office and everything. And you should see all the paperwork. There are mountains of it! He took me on a special tour to see the column and I met the seller, a very distinguished gentleman who told me how sad he was to be selling Nelson's Column.'

Lady Chichester put down her soup spoon. 'I'm afraid it sounds like an elaborate hoax,' she said. 'A landmark like Nelson's Column belongs to the nation. It's owned by the state. The government. The King. I don't know exactly who, but someone like that. What I'm trying to say is it belongs to the entire country. You don't just have a man who owns it then sells it to you via a broker. I think Mr Jones has pocketed your twenty thousand pounds and probably gave a little bit to the man who was pretending to be the owner.'

'No, Lady Chichester. You've got it all wrong,' said Mrs

Stanley-Piggot. 'I know it's nice to believe these landmarks are owned by the nation. But they're simply not. It's the way of the world these days. I've got the deeds and everything.'

'Did you consult a solicitor when you bought the column?' asked Lord Chichester.

'Yes.'

'And the solicitor said the sale was genuine, did he?'

'Yes, he did.'

'How did you find the solicitor?'

'Mr Jones recommended him. I was going to use my own solicitor, but Mr Jones's solicitor offered me a very good deal, so I went with him instead.'

Mr Lawrence laughed and Mrs Stanley-Piggot gave him a sharp glance.

'Oh good grief,' said Miss Darby. 'Can't you see that he would have been in on the trick, too? This is an entire team of people who have conned you out of an awful lot of money, Mrs Stanley-Piggot. You should go to the police about this.'

'Nonsense. And even if I have been conned, do you think the police will be interested if I tell them I've accidentally bought Nelson's Column? No. I must say that you're quite ruining my day, Miss Darby. I've been very excited about this purchase and now my feelings are hurt.'

Chapter Nine

After dinner, Lord Chichester suggested a stroll in the gardens as the guests for the evening performances and dancing arrived.

'It's a lovely spot here, isn't it, Lottie?' said Mrs Moore. They strolled past the tall hedges of the maze and followed the path towards an ornate fountain. 'The guests are intriguing. I can't say I warm to the Lawrences very much and that poor Mrs Stanley-Piggot clearly has more money than sense. Oh look.' She raised her lorgnette. 'Is that Daisy Darby over there?'

A slender young woman in a powder blue gown lingered by the fountain smoking a cigarette.

'She's quite a serious lady, isn't she? Let's see if we can cheer her up.'

Rosie trotted up to Miss Darby and the young woman greeted her with a pat.

'Hello Miss Darby!' said Mrs Moore. 'Enjoying a quiet moment?'

'Yes.'

'I'm sorry we've ruined it for you.'

'Oh, don't be sorry at all. It's quite alright.'

'Are you performing this evening?'

'Yes, Ruby and I are doing a rendition of *Always Remember Your Brolly On An English Summer's Day.*'

'That sounds like good advice. Is it one of Mr Lawrence's songs?'

'We're only ever allowed to sing Mr Lawrence's songs.' Miss Darby curled her lip.

'I see. You'd like to sing other songs too?'

'Yes, I would. But we've signed a contract with him, so we have to stick to it.'

'Ah yes, contracts can be tricky things, can't they?'

'You read through a contract thinking everything looks fine. Then after you've signed it, you realise it has all these restrictions you never noticed before.'

'So you're unhappy with it?'

'Yes.'

'But presumably you enjoy performing in the Pom-Pom Duo.'

There was a pause. Daisy inhaled on her cigarette.

'I used to,' she said eventually. 'But things have changed and I can't say I enjoy it as much anymore.'

'Oh no! Why not?'

'Well...' She glanced around her to check there was no one else about. 'You won't tell anyone else this, will you?'

'No, we promise not to tell, don't we, Lottie?'

Lottie nodded, keen to hear more.

'Ruby and I first met as chorus girls,' said Daisy. 'Some people still describe us as chorus girls, but we're not anymore. We're a performing duo now, but back then we were just two girls in a line-up of thirty dancers. We all wore matching outfits and danced in a line, side-by-side, one behind the other, that sort of thing. It was quite good fun, but Ruby and I wanted to perform on our own. So that's when we began as the Pom-Pom Duo. We wanted to wear colourful costumes and sing fun, happy songs while shaking pom-poms. We put together some dances and songs, and eventually we found a manager who agreed to take us on. He wasn't very well-connected, but he managed to get us a few performances in music halls. It was during one of those performances when Mr Lawrence spotted us.'

'Mr Lawrence went to a music hall?' said Mrs Moore. 'I'm sure his wife would be horrified.'

'She doesn't like music halls or chorus girls, does she? Anyway, I think the main reason Mr Lawrence spotted us was Ruby.'

'And you.'

'No. He's always preferred Ruby. He only begrudgingly took me on because she insisted on it. Anyway, Mr Lawrence worked wonders for our careers. We began at the bottom of the bill, but within eighteen months, we were in the middle. And then we had a show when we were top billing! It was very exciting.'

'Was? It's not exciting anymore?'

'It's changing. There's talk now of us becoming a trio and being called Lady Chichester and the Pom-Poms.'

'Oh dear, I don't like that name.'

'I'm pleased to hear it because I don't either! I don't want another girl to join us and I also don't want Ruby standing at the front taking all the credit.'

'And this is Mr Lawrence's plan?'

'Yes. Ruby's all for it, of course. But I'm not. I can see why Mr Lawrence prefers Ruby, she's far prettier than me.'

'Is she?'

'Oh yes. She has a pretty nose and better ankles. And she gets the better costumes too. We used to wear matching outfits, but Mr Lawrence decided we should wear things which reflect our personalities. So Ruby always wears better colours and has more sequins and feathers than me.'

'That doesn't sound fair.'

'It's not! And it's got worse since Ruby became Lady Chichester.'

'How did she meet Lord Chichester?'

'He saw us perform at the Empire Theatre and visited our dressing room backstage. Ruby immediately took an interest in him, even though he was married and Ruby was courting the impresario Mr Romano.'

'Lady Chichester was courting another gentleman at the time?'

'Yes. But she was so impressed with Lord Chichester that she left Mr Romano. And then the first Lady Chichester found out about it and the divorce happened. As soon as it had been finalised, Ruby married him! She couldn't wait to become Lady Chichester and get her hands on this place. Who wouldn't? Just look at it.' She gestured at their impressive surroundings. 'Ruby's a member of the landed gentry now. Her father worked on the railways and she was born in Bermondsey! It doesn't seem right.'

'She's certainly done a good job of climbing the social ladder,' said Mrs Moore.

Miss Darby checked her watch. 'Oops, look at the time. I'd better go and get ready.'

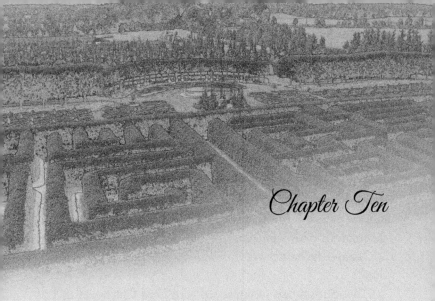

LOTTIE, Mrs Moore and Rosie made their way to the ballroom for the evening's entertainment. The room had been decorated with streamers, balloons and flower displays in enormous vases. A stage stood at one end and a band was positioned to the right of it. Well-dressed guests were filling the lines of chairs which had been set out for the audience.

They came across Mrs Stanley-Piggot looking for somewhere to sit.

'I need a small person to sit behind,' she explained. 'I can see around a small person with no problem at all. But there's nothing worse than making yourself comfortable somewhere only for a tall person in a top hat to place themselves in front of you. It ruins the entire evening.'

'I couldn't agree more,' said Mrs Moore. Eventually they found three suitable seats and sat down. Lottie was sandwiched between Mrs Moore and Mrs Stanley-Piggot with Rosie on her lap.

Lord Chichester climbed onto the stage with a glass of port in his hand. He bowed to the resulting applause. 'Good evening my distinguished guests!' he began. 'My dear wife and

I are immensely grateful for your company this evening to help us celebrate the occasion of our first wedding anniversary!'

This was met with more applause.

'I'm happy to inform you that you'll be seeing a good deal of my wife in this evening's performances. But before we get to those, I've received a request from Captain Brownlees to explain a little more about the history of my beautiful home. I get asked an awful lot of questions about it and it makes sense, while I'm standing up here in front of you all, to give you a quick potted history. It saves me having to repeat myself later!'

'I've heard it all before,' Mrs Stanley-Piggot whispered to Lottie. 'Francis and I were regular visitors here for years.'

'I'll begin by saying I consider myself a fortunate man,' continued Lord Chichester. 'I was born into this world without the tiniest inkling I would inherit an estate like this. The earliest Hamilton Hall is believed to have been built in the fourteenth century. The place burned down a few times and each time it was built back bigger and better than before. That's what us Chichesters are like! Few of you will remember the previous Lord Chichester, he was a reclusive chap. He had no immediate family of his own and had little to do with the wider Chichester family. He just rattled about this place like a dried-up old pea in a concert hall and kept himself to himself.'

Lottie wondered why Lord Chichester had made the assumption everyone was interested in his story.

'Meanwhile, I grew up in southwest London in a reasonably well-to-do family,' he continued. 'My family was affluent, but we had no idea my great uncle had this place. We knew of his existence and that he lived up here in Buckinghamshire, but we never visited him. He never invited anyone, you see. He quite removed himself from the rest of the family. My grandfather was his brother and the sixth son of the then-Lord Chichester. He didn't inherit much at all. His family had to pretty much make their own way in life. So that's what we did! And we're proud of it!'

Applause rang out and Lord Chichester held up his glass to call for silence.

'My great uncle, however, owned this place. He was my grandfather's eldest brother. The firstborn son. That's why everything went to him. I suppose the family assumed my great uncle would marry and have an heir of his own. But that never happened. And can you believe that the only one of his brothers who had an heir was my grandfather? My great uncle reached the grand old age of ninety-five. He outlived my grandfather and my father. So on his death, who do you think was the beneficiary?'

The audience chuckled.

'That's right. It was me! So there I was, leading my own merry life, going to Harrow and then Oxford, and then I went off to fight in the Second Boer War. A terrible time it was. My parents both died while I was away fighting, and that was very difficult. I came back a changed man. So you can imagine my surprise when I heard I had inherited this grand estate. Although, this place was quite a wreck when I came to see it. It needed an awful lot of work doing to it, and I'm afraid to say I had to sell some of the family treasures in order to pay for the work.

'And if it wasn't for me marrying, then the Chichester family name would have died out! Once you have a title such as Lord Chichester, then you're eligible to marry into some of the great families of this country. When word spread that I was an eligible young bachelor who had inherited the Chichester estate, many families were clamouring for me to marry their daughters. I pretty much had my pick of the lot. The Forbes family were the successful bidders.' He gave a chuckle. 'We had some happy years of marriage and produced an heir and three spares. And now I've found another beautiful wife! I really couldn't be luckier.'

Everyone clapped and cheered, but Lottie couldn't help thinking he was a little too smug.

'Anyway, that's enough about me,' said Lord Chichester. 'Let's get on with the show. Please welcome on stage the delightful Pom-Pom Duo!'

Chapter Eleven

THE BAND STRUCK up a lively tune. Then two performers in sequinned dresses skipped onto the stage. Lady Chichester and Miss Darby. They both carried umbrellas trimmed with pom-poms for *Always Remember Your Brolly On An English Summer's Day*.

It was a well-rehearsed routine with matching dance steps in perfect synchronicity. When they reached the jaunty chorus, the duo twirled their colourful umbrellas and Lottie felt her foot tapping along.

There was little doubt that Lady Chichester wore the better costume. Her sherbet-pink dress was completely covered in sequins while Miss Darby's pale blue dress was only partially covered by them.

After hearing Miss Darby's lament about the Pom-Pom Duo, Lottie wondered what the outcome would be. Presumably it was difficult for Miss Darby to leave because of the contract she had signed.

The performance ended and there were whoops and applause from the audience. Quentin Lawrence took to the stage and performed a deep bow so everyone could thank him for the song.

'And now we have another treat for us,' he said. 'My dear wife, Maria, will perform an extract from the Scottish play!'

The audience clapped as Mrs Lawrence walked onto the stage. She wore a crown on a red wig with two long plaits which hung down to her knees. Her green medieval-style dress was embroidered with beads and had enormous winged sleeves. Lottie had seen pictures of the famous actress Ellen Terry as Lady Macbeth, and it seemed that Maria Lawrence had copied her exactly. Everyone listened intently as Mrs Lawrence raised her crown above her head and began her soliloquy. It was a dramatic, emotional performance and Lottie wasn't sure what the speech actually meant. But Maria received a lot of appreciation at the end.

A man with a boater hat and a walking cane sang some amusing ditties and Rosie grew restless. Lottie realised she needed to take her out into the garden for a short walk. She managed to quietly squeeze along the row and get out as a singer in a tangerine outfit was taking to the stage.

Fortunately, the tall doors of the ballroom stood open out onto the garden. It was a mild spring evening, and the sun was lowering in the sky. Lottie felt tempted to investigate the maze in front of her. But what if she struggled to find her way out? She didn't want to be lost in the maze when she was supposed to be watching the performances with Mrs Moore. Rosie sniffed at an urn on the terrace and Lottie began to walk along the side of the house. She passed the ballroom and reached a window which was propped open. She was about to pass it when she heard voices.

Chapter Twelve

'I've told you before about stressing the right syllable in the word summer, Ruby. You need to draw out the second syllable of the word so it fits with the tune.'

'Oh Quentin, you're so fussy. It's my wedding anniversary! And my house! I'll perform the song how I want to!'

Lottie paused near the open window and listened some more.

'Not when you're performing with another person and a band,' said Mr Lawrence's voice. 'It can be very off-putting for them. And you came in too early with the heel-toe during the chorus. How many times have we practised that? It's a careless mistake.'

'Well, it was probably the champagne I had during dinner. I rarely drink champagne before a performance, Quentin. You know me. I'm impeccably behaved. But I think you're being terribly fussy because it's not as if we're in the West End this evening.'

'And thank goodness we're not! Can you imagine the reception you'd have received if you'd put on that performance at the Gaiety?'

'I can't believe how picky you are, Quentin! The audience barely noticed my mistakes. Why aren't you telling Daisy off, too?'

'Because she's not as important as you are, Ruby.'

'Oh nonsense! You're just pernickety and fussy. And I've had enough of it. I've a good mind to stop doing this altogether.'

'You can't!'

'Yes, I can.'

'You wouldn't dare. And don't forget my songs are the reason you're famous.'

'It's not just your songs. Anybody could sing your songs and get nowhere. The reason I'm famous is I have talent!'

'Talent is useless if you don't have the right song. You can't do this without me. And I'm a perfectionist, I'm afraid. I put a lot of work into my songs and I like to see them performed in the way I intended.'

'You've put a lot of work into your songs? Don't make me laugh, Quentin. I know where you got them from.'

'That's enough! Every songwriter is inspired by others.'

'Inspired? I call it—'

'Shush! Can't you see the window is open?'

Lottie took a step away from it in case one of them looked out.

'No one is out there. They're all listening to Mrs Patterson ruin *Let's Go To The Races*.'

'Well, you could learn a few lessons from her, Ruby. Now you need to prepare yourself for the closing number. Don't forget I'm in that one with you.'

'And I suppose you're going to have words with me about that when it's done, aren't you? You're a bully, Quentin. I'm going to tell William all about you.'

'You can try it, Ruby. But I don't think he'll be very cross with me. Your husband doesn't understand the first thing about show business, so I think he'll be happy to defer to me on that matter. I've worked in this industry for thirty years. I know what the standard needs to be.'

'Well, if you don't stop bullying me, I shall tell people where you got your songs from.'

'You wouldn't!'

'Oh yes I would. I'm Lady Chichester now. It doesn't matter to me if this silly career comes to an end. But if your career came to an end, Quentin, you would mind very much, wouldn't you?'

LOTTIE RETURNED to the ballroom as a magician on the stage was pulling a bunch of flowers from his sleeve. The last performance was then announced. Lady Chichester and Mr Lawrence performing his song, *I Lost My Heart to a Sailor on the High, High Seas*.

Lottie gulped. How were they going to manage it after their argument? And she couldn't stop thinking about the apparent threat Lady Chichester had made. Where had Quentin Lawrence got his songs from and was she going to tell all?

Lady Chichester strolled onto the stage in a lacy cream gown. The song was a lovelorn ballad and, as she sang, Mr Lawrence appeared in a sailor's costume. Lottie stifled a laugh, thinking he looked quite comical. It wasn't supposed to be a comical performance, though. Lady Chichester moved whimsically around the stage and Mr Lawrence followed her about, looking love-struck.

Lottie felt her toes curl.

'Boo!' came a lady's voice from the back. 'This is rubbish!' There were gasps in the audience as people turned around to see the heckler. The band continued to play, but Lady Chichester stopped singing and buried her face in her hands. Then she ran off the stage and Mr Lawrence followed her.

'Absolute rubbish!' repeated the woman. Lottie craned her head to see a middle-aged lady with grey bobbed hair. She wore a smart burgundy dress and two footmen were by her side, encouraging her to leave.

'Oh dear, it's the first Lady Chichester,' said a woman close by.

'So it is!' said Mrs Moore. 'I recognise her now.'

'This marriage is a sham!' called out Lady Forbes-Chichester. 'She only married him for his money and a title!' The footmen tried to take her arms, but she shrugged them off.

The band stopped and Lord Chichester clambered onto the stage, port slopping out of his glass. 'Nothing to worry about, everyone! It appears an interloper has joined us.'

'Interloper? I was your first wife! And you left me for that chorus girl!'

Lord Chichester gave an uncomfortable laugh.

'May I invite everyone to step outside on this lovely evening? We just need to remove someone from the ballroom. But please do return in twenty minutes or so, and everything will be ready for this evening's dances.'

THE GUESTS SPILLED out onto the terrace, chatting enthusiastically about the evening's drama. The sun was low in the sky, and dusk was approaching.

Maria Lawrence joined Lottie and Mrs Moore. She was still dressed as Lady Macbeth.

'Congratulations on your wonderful performance,' said Mrs Moore.

'Thank you. I'm relieved it wasn't interrupted by Lord Chichester's first wife. What an embarrassment that was. I suppose they've only got themselves to blame.'

'What do you mean by that?' asked Mrs Moore.

'This is what happens when a lord marries a chorus girl. Although Lord and Lady Chichester are probably very happy together, there's no doubt she was initially drawn to him because of his wealth and status. It's a fact of life, I'm afraid. I'm fortunate enough to be comfortable with who I am. But some women are easily impressed, especially those from simple backgrounds. They go after these rich men and they have no idea what trouble they're storing up for themselves. It seems Daisy Darby is trying to repeat Lady Chichester's success.

There are rumours about her and Lord Moorcroft at the moment.'

'Lord Moorcroft?' said Mrs Moore. 'I know him. That's quite shocking. I thought he was such a devoted family man.'

'They often are. And then they meet a young, attractive chorus girl and get rather distracted. Most of the time, it's little more than a dalliance. Although in Lord Chichester's case, he decided to go through a divorce and actually marry her. Perhaps there is some genuine love there between them and I shouldn't be so judgemental.'

'Perhaps Daisy Darby needs to find herself a respectable bachelor her own age,' said Mrs Moore.

'Yes, I think so. I took her to one side and gave her that advice. She didn't appreciate it, of course. She's probably too young to realise what's good for her. But I explained to her she's in danger of getting a terrible reputation if she keeps going after wealthy married men. She's reached the point where she has to either stop it or marry someone respectable.'

'Yes, that makes sense,' said Mrs Moore.

'I suppose if you've been born into a family with little money, the lure of power and wealth is intoxicating.'

'I suppose it must be.'

'It's rather like consuming a large box of chocolates. It's tempting at the time and you thoroughly enjoy yourself. But in the long run, it's no good for your waistline, is it?'

'I say,' announced a red-faced man close by. 'Who fancies a wander in the maze?'

'Don't be silly, Rupert,' said his lady companion. 'You'll never find your way out again.'

'Ten shillings says I will! I'll find the centre and get out again within five minutes.'

'Sounds like a challenge,' said a lean man with grey whiskers. 'What do you say, Edwina?'

'I'm game!' replied his companion.

They headed off and other people got the same idea. Within a minute, a stream of guests was heading for the maze entrance.

'Look at us being a herd of sheep!' laughed Mrs Stanley-Piggot as she passed by.

'Well, it wouldn't do any harm, would it?' said Mrs Lawrence. 'I don't know where my husband's got to. Consoling Lady Chichester somewhere, I expect.' She followed Mrs Stanley-Piggot.

'It's something to do, isn't it, Lottie?' said Mrs Moore. 'And I've found my way out of this maze before. I feel sure I can remember the way.'

Chapter Fifteen

THE NARROW PATHWAYS of the maze were filled with excitable guests. The evening light was fading, and the neatly clipped hedge walls towered ten feet over everyone's heads. Lottie clipped the lead onto Rosie's collar so she could keep her dog close. She didn't want her getting lost.

People jostled each other while saying "Excuse me" and "I do beg your pardon." Giggling ladies squeezed past with drinks in their hands, and smartly dressed gentlemen tripped over people's heels as they tried to race each other to the centre.

'I'm regretting this already, Lottie,' said Mrs Moore. 'The maze looks different when it's filled with people.' They rounded a corner and found themselves in a crowd at a standstill.

'Go back! Go back!' shouted a man with a bushy moustache. 'It's a dead end!'

'Let's turn around and go the way we came,' said someone.

Lottie and Mrs Moore turned around and tried to find

another route. Around them, they could hear the voices of people losing their patience.

'How on earth does one get out of this thing?' came a man's voice from the other side of the hedge.

'Has anyone found the centre yet?' asked another.

They turned left and right and left and right and the effect was dizzying after a while. Lottie kept coming across the same people and couldn't understand why no one was making any progress. Her enthusiasm began to wane.

'Goodness, my feet are hurting in these shoes, Lottie,' said Mrs Moore. 'I didn't anticipate walking like this. How much distance do you think we've covered? It feels like three miles.'

'You're right, it does feel like that.'

The light grew dimmer, and eventually they heard encouraging voices from the other side of the hedge. 'Hooray! Here's the centre!'

'We're close to it, Lottie!' Mrs Moore quickened her step and Lottie followed as they turned left and right and left and right. But the closer they tried to get to the centre, the further they found themselves away from it.

Lottie wished they had never set foot in the maze, and it seemed that most of the people around them thought the same too.

'Oh dear. I feel quite dizzy now,' said Mrs Moore. 'It's getting dark. I'm worried we're going to be stuck in here all night!'

They turned left and found themselves in the centre of the maze. It was a small, enclosed space with a statue in the middle.

'Oh. Well, here we are then,' said Mrs Moore. 'I suppose we should celebrate, but I feel too tired, Lottie.'

They were joined by the red-faced man whose idea it had been to enter the maze. 'Thank goodness for that,' he said. 'The centre. Although I'll be far happier when I find the exit.'

'It looks like you've lost your ten-shilling bet,' said Mrs Moore.

'Yes, I think I lost it about half an hour ago. I've lost my friends too. This maze strips you of everything. Can you remember the way back?'

'I'm afraid not. Even though I've found my way out of here before.'

'Have you? Oh dear, there really is no hope, is there?' He surveyed the statue. 'Is that Lady Chichester?'

'Yes, that's what the plaque on it says.'

'If only she could tell us the way out! Oh well, I'd better get on with it. See you on the other side.'

The red-faced man left.

'The centre of the maze is an anti-climax really, isn't it, Lottie?'

Lottie nodded. 'And we've still got to find our way out. I'm worried it's going to get too dark.'

More people arrived, but their reactions to reaching the centre were muted. Everyone looked exhausted. Then the lean man with grey whiskers appeared.

'Oh no, not the centre again!' he fumed. 'No matter how much I try to find the exit, I end up back here!'

'Why not try to find the centre and perhaps you'll then find the exit?' said Lottie.

He thought about this for a moment. 'Now that's an ingenious idea, young lady. I'll give it a go.'

'We'll follow,' said Mrs Moore. The lean, whiskered man was a fast walker, and they had to jog to keep up with him. Then they came across a clump of people having a rest. By the time Lottie had got past them, it was too late to see if Mrs Moore and the whiskered man had gone right or left.

'Oh dear Rosie,' she said. 'We've lost them. It looks like we'll have to work this out between us. Which way looks right to you?'

Chapter Sixteen

LOTTIE AND ROSIE plodded through the maze, unsure of where they were heading. They turned a corner and bumped into Quentin Lawrence. He was still dressed in his sailor costume.

'Hello Miss Sprigg, have you seen my wife anywhere?'

'I saw her enter the maze, but I've not seen her since.'

'Oh bother. I came in here to find her. Perhaps she's already escaped. I'll head back out again.'

'It's tricky to get out, we're trying to do the same.'

'Nonsense, it's easy. It's this way.' He marched off and Lottie decided not to follow. The thought of being trapped in a maze with him was unappealing.

Lottie continued on her way with Rosie and encountered more lost guests. It wasn't long before she saw Mr Lawrence again. He seemed embarrassed about it.

'I took a wrong turn, but it's alright. I know where I went wrong.' He dashed off again.

A moment later, Mrs Stanley-Piggot appeared. 'I'm trying to follow Mr Lawrence, but he's too quick for me,' she said. 'Apparently, he knows the way out.'

'He went that way,' said Lottie, pointing in the direction she'd last seen him.

'Oh thank you, Miss Sprigg.'

Lottie felt sure that Mr Lawrence knew no better than she did, so she persevered with following her own route. 'We'll get there Rosie, I know it.'

'Hello!' came a lady's voice from around the corner.

It was Lady Chichester.

'Hello,' she said to Lottie. 'Are you lost?'

'Very.'

'This maze is a devil to get out of, isn't it? But don't worry, William and I are here to save everyone now. You're actually quite near the exit now.'

'Am I? Thank goodness.'

'From here you need to go right, right, left, right again, then left, then right.'

Lottie took in a breath as she tried to remember this. 'Right, right, left, right, left, right,' she repeated.

'Perfect. Do you think you can remember it?'

'Yes, I'll remember.'

'Well done. I'd better go and rescue the others.'

Lady Chichester walked on and Lottie repeated the directions in her head as she made her way through the last section of the maze.

She stopped at a crossroads. 'Oh dear, which way is it, Rosie? Right, right, left, right, left, right. I think we've done the third right, so it's left here.'

Lottie couldn't control her relief when she finally saw the exit in the hedge. She laughed and felt tearful all at the same time.

'We're out, Rosie! We're out!'

It was almost dark. The terrace was lit with lanterns and the guests who'd escaped the maze lingered there, waiting for companions to emerge. The man with the bushy moustache staggered out of the maze after Lottie. 'Good grief,' he said. 'I think we all deserve a medal for that!'

Lottie looked around for Mrs Moore. She would be easy to spot in her enormous plum-purple gown.

Eventually she found her, weary and limping along the terrace. She gave Lottie a tired grin as she approached.

'You're safe, Lottie!'

'Yes, I'm pleased to be out of there.'

'Me too. What an ordeal! But we survived it. We lived to tell the tale and—'

She was interrupted by a scream.

It cut through the evening air and made Lottie's blood run cold.

It was followed by a horrible silence before a voice cried out.

'Murder! Help!'

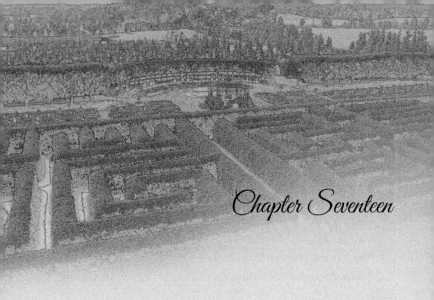

Chapter Seventeen

'THE CRY for help is coming from the maze!' said Mrs Moore.

'Someone call the police!' shouted the man with the bushy moustache. 'And a doctor!'

'I'm a doctor,' said a woman in a sunflower-yellow dress.

'You're a doctor?'

'Yes. A lady doctor. Is there something wrong with that?'

'No. Nothing wrong with that. It sounds like they need help in there.' He pointed at the maze and the doctor dashed towards it with some other people in tow.

Lottie bit her lip, anxious that it would take them a while to find the scene of the tragedy.

Staff ushered the guests into the ballroom where the chairs had been cleared out of the way for the evening's dancing.

'I can't quite believe it,' said Mrs Moore. 'We were having such fun, and now... Actually we weren't having very much fun. That escapade in the maze was a bit much. And it appears to have ended very badly for someone. A murder in a maze, Lottie? It doesn't seem real, does it?'

Lottie shook her head. It didn't seem real at all.

'We only went into the maze because the evening was interrupted by Lady Forbes-Chichester,' continued Mrs Moore. 'If she hadn't heckled Lady Chichester's performance, then we would have all remained here in the ballroom and begun the dances. Look, the band members are packing their instruments away. It really has ended rather horribly, hasn't it?'

Mr and Mrs Lawrence entered the ballroom with pale faces. Their sailor and Lady Macbeth costumes seemed out of place now. Lottie realised she'd escaped the maze before Mr Lawrence had. Was it possible he'd seen or heard something of the murder?

'Oh, thank goodness the pair of you are alright.' They turned to see Mrs Stanley-Piggot. 'I'm trying to work out who's missing,' she said, looking around. 'There are a lot of guests here, so it's difficult to tell. Oh, I can see the Lawrences now, that's good. Where are Lord and Lady Chichester?'

'I don't know,' said Mrs Moore. 'I haven't seen them. I hope they're not caught up in the tragedy.'

'It seems that some unfortunate soul is,' said Mrs Stanley-Piggot. 'I can only hope that cry of murder was a mistake.'

'It sounded quite certain to me,' said Mrs Moore. 'I'm not sure how anyone could be mistaken about such a thing.'

'We gathered here for a happy event,' said Mrs Stanley-Piggot with a sigh. 'And it's all gone so horribly wrong. The band is packing up I see and all these beautiful decorations are here for nothing.' She reached out to a nearby flower arrangement and cradled a rose in her hand. 'Oh! Ouch!' She withdrew her hand and pushed her finger into her mouth.

'Did you prick yourself, Mrs Stanley-Piggot?'

'I'm afraid I did. That's the trouble with roses, isn't it? Quite beautiful, but rather prickly too.'

The room fell silent and Lottie saw why. Lord Chichester

stood in the doorway, his expression stricken. He planted a foot forward as though it were a struggle to bear his own weight. Then he stopped and gazed around the room, as if he was only seeing it now for the first time.

'It brings me enormous sadness to inform you all that my dear wife... my darling wife, Ruby... is dead!'

Chapter Eighteen

THE CHAIRS WERE SET out in the ballroom again so everyone had somewhere to sit as they waited for the police to arrive. The staff began taking down the decorations and removing the flower displays.

Lottie, Rosie and Mrs Moore sat on a pair of chairs by a wall. 'So Lady Chichester has been murdered in the maze,' said Mrs Moore. 'There can't have been many people left in there at the time of her death.'

'I saw her in there,' said Lottie. 'She showed me the way out. Then she went off to help other guests.'

'Was she on her own at the time?'

'Yes. And she seemed fine. I don't understand how someone managed to murder her about five minutes later.'

Mrs Moore blew out a sigh. 'Awful.'

'I'm sure Quentin Lawrence was still in the maze when I got out. And I saw Mrs Stanley-Piggot in there too. She was trying to follow him.'

'You think they were both still in the maze at the time of the murder?'

'Yes. And Lady Chichester told me she and her husband

53

were in the maze helping the guests find their way out. So he must have been in there too.'

'Interesting. It sounds like there's a shortlist of suspects already.'

'Oh no, I wouldn't want to consider them suspects just yet. There were some other guests in the maze too.'

'Including the person who let out that blood-curdling scream. Presumably she was the person who found Lady Chichester.'

'I said I wouldn't want to consider any suspects yet,' said Lottie. 'However, I overheard an argument between Lady Chichester and Quentin Lawrence after her first performance.'

'Did you? How?'

'When Rosie got restless, and I took her out for a quick walk along the terrace. A window was open, and I heard the argument.

'Mr Lawrence was being very picky about Lady Chichester's performance. He was pointing out mistakes she'd made and said she hadn't done it very well.'

'Golly, that sounds rather harsh.'

'I felt a bit sorry for her when I heard him say that.'

'And what did she say to him?'

'She sounded angry and upset. And quite rightly, I think. And she told him she knew where his songs came from.'

'What does that mean?'

'I don't know. I heard her say that she knew where his songs came from and that she could tell people. She also said she didn't care about her career ending, but he would care if his career came to an end.'

'That suggests she knew something which could ruin his reputation as a songwriter. I wonder what it was? Golly, Lottie, I think you could have identified a motive. But would Quentin Lawrence do such a thing?'

Chapter Nineteen

DETECTIVE INSPECTOR WILSON stood on the ballroom stage with his hands in his pockets. He surveyed the guests sitting in front of him with narrow eyes. 'This is a grave matter indeed,' he said. 'A young lady attacked through a hedge while speaking to a friend.'

'Attacked through a hedge?' Mrs Moore whispered to Lottie. 'How does someone do that?'

The detective pulled a notebook from his pocket. 'Miss Darby,' he said. 'Perhaps you could tell us all exactly what happened.'

Daisy Darby sat red-eyed on a chair near the stage. 'It was horrible!' She gave a sniff.

'These things usually are. But we need your account.'

'Very well.' She wiped her nose with her handkerchief. 'I was lost in the maze, just like everyone else. I couldn't find my way out. And then Ruby found me.'

'You mean Lady Chichester.'

'Yes. I called her Ruby because we were good friends. I was very relieved when she found me.'

'And did you have a conversation?'

'Yes. She said she'd show me the way out and then she told me that...' She stopped and glanced around the room.

'What did she tell you about, Miss Darby?'

'She told me that Mr Lawrence had said some mean things to her after our performance this evening.'

'What sort of things?'

'Comments about her singing and dancing and she said she'd had enough of it.'

'Excuse me!' Quentin Lawrence rose out of his seat. 'It's unfair painting me as the villain in all this!'

'No one's painting you as anything, Mr Lawrence,' said the detective. 'We need to hear Miss Darby's account.'

'When do I get my say?'

'When I ask you for it.'

Mrs Lawrence tugged on her husband's sailor shirt to encourage him to sit down again. The detective turned back to Miss Darby. 'What else did Lady Chichester say?'

'There wasn't much else. Because that's when it happened.'

'What happened?'

'I'd just asked her for more detail about what Mr Lawrence had said to her and she just stood there staring at me. I was about to ask her what was wrong when she gave out a cry and fell to the floor. That's when I saw the knife. Oh, it was just horrible!' She buried her face in her hands.

'So the atrocity was committed by someone on the other side of the hedge?'

There was a pause as Miss Darby recovered herself. 'Yes. A hand came through the hedge with the knife.'

'Did you see the hand?'

'No. Because Ruby was standing in the way. I didn't see any hand at all. I just saw the knife. And I realised that someone could only have done it by pushing their hand through the hedge.' She gave a shudder. 'It was barbaric.

Someone must have been listening to our conversation on the other side of the hedge. And that's when they decided to do it!'

'May I say something, Detective?' Lord Chichester got to his feet. 'We only have Miss Darby's word that this happened. How do we know she didn't commit the crime herself?'

'I didn't!' wailed Miss Darby.

'You were envious of Ruby's success,' said Lord Chichester. 'And you wanted the limelight for yourself!'

'No, I didn't!' said Daisy. 'We were both successful, why would I be envious of Ruby?'

Lottie recalled Miss Darby grumbling that Mr Lawrence preferred Lady Chichester over her. Was it possible that jealousy had prompted her to murder her friend?

'With my wife out of the way, you can claim all the attention for yourself!' continued Lord Chichester. 'You can be the Pom-Pom... I don't know. Pom-Pom Lady or something. I don't know.'

'How ridiculous! Why would I ever want that for myself? And besides, I think it was Mr Lawrence on the other side of that hedge.'

'Me?' Quentin Lawrence jumped to his feet again.

'Ruby was complaining to me about you, and I think you wanted to silence her.'

Chapter Twenty

'ABSOLUTE NONSENSE!' said Quentin Lawrence. 'I had no desire to silence Ruby Chichester. And besides, I wasn't even in the maze at that time.'

'Yes you were,' said Mrs Stanley-Piggot. 'I was following you because you told me you knew how to get out. It turned out you didn't know at all.'

'If you were following me, Mrs Stanley-Piggot, then you would surely have seen me poke a knife through a hedge. But you didn't, did you? I have an alibi, Detective!'

'I couldn't keep up with you,' said Mrs Stanley-Piggot. 'So I lost sight of you shortly before the murder happened.'

'Lord Chichester was also in the maze,' said Mr Lawrence. 'Why is no one accusing him?'

'How dare you stand under my roof as my guest and accuse me of murdering my wife!' roared Lord Chichester.

Mr Lawrence pulled a grimace, clearly regretting his accusation.

'And I want to hear more about what you were saying to Ruby after her performance, Lawrence,' continued Lord

Chichester. 'She told Miss Darby that you were criticising her singing and dancing.'

'It was the usual post-performance critique, my lord. I'm a perfectionist, everyone knows that. And it's quite natural to go over what worked and what didn't work once the performance is complete. It was nothing.'

'Ruby didn't act like it was nothing,' said Miss Darby. 'In fact, she was quite upset by it.'

'Well, obviously I regret upsetting Ruby, it certainly wasn't my intention. She was probably exaggerating a bit.'

Lottie felt her heart thud as she realised she had some useful information to impart. Cautiously, she raised her hand.

'Yes, young lady?' said the detective.

'I overheard some of the conversation between Mr Lawrence and Lady Chichester,' she said.

'Go on,' said the detective.

Lottie felt all the eyes in the room on her as she recounted what she'd heard.

'Does that sound accurate, Mr Lawrence?' asked the detective once Lottie had finished.

'Sort of.' He gave a sniff. 'I think it makes me sound angrier than I actually was, though.'

'What did Lady Chichester mean when she said she was going to tell people where your songs came from?' asked the detective.

'Oh, that was just a little joke between us.'

'A joke? There doesn't appear to have been much joviality in your conversation.'

'If Miss Sprigg had stayed to eavesdrop a little longer, then she would have heard us both laughing afterwards.'

'Laughing?'

'Yes. It's embarrassing to admit this, Detective, but in the very early stages of my career, I had a little help with my song writing.'

'Who helped you?'

'Well, this is the amusing bit. My mother!' He gave a chuckle, but no one in the room joined in with him.

'Your mother helped write your songs?'

'In the very, very early stages of my career. And we're talking years ago now, Detective. I once shared that confession with Ruby and she thought it was very funny. She even said she would tell people my mother wrote all my songs!' He laughed again but this time it was uneasy.

Detective Inspector Wilson gave a baffled sigh and wrote something in his notebook.

'So from what we can glean, the assailant heard Lady Chichester and Miss Darby in conversation while on the other side of the hedge. The assailant then chose that moment to strike. They cleverly hid behind the screening which a tall hedge provides. And after they committed the atrocity, they went on their way and pretended to be another guest lost in the maze. There is only one way in and out of the maze, so they must have passed through without anyone noticing anything amiss. It was very cunning indeed. But that doesn't mean we won't find them, whoever they are. Clues will have been left.'

'What sort of clues?' asked Lord Chichester. 'The assailant plunged a knife through a hedge, then walked away. Have you dusted the knife for fingerprints?'

'My men are working on it right now. But if the assailant wore gloves, then it may be difficult to retrieve anything.'

'So there could be no clues at all then, Detective? This is the sort of crime someone could easily get away with!'

Chapter Twenty-One

DETECTIVE INSPECTOR WILSON asked to interview everyone in turn. Fortunately for Lottie and Mrs Moore, they were among the first to be summoned. It was almost eleven o'clock in the evening as they sat in comfortable chairs in the saffron-yellow morning room with the detective and a police sergeant called Travers.

'I'm impressed by your eavesdropping skills, Miss Sprigg,' said the detective. 'Have you ever thought about becoming a detective?'

'No, I haven't,' she said. 'But I do like detective stories. And thank you for the compliment.'

'Give it some consideration.' He pointed his pen at her. 'Years ago, men scoffed at the idea of lady detectives, but some are successfully setting themselves up as private eyes these days. I can tell you have a sharp mind.'

Lottie blushed, embarrassed by the praise.

'She does indeed,' said Mrs Moore. 'That's why I employed her.'

Lottie distracted herself by patting Rosie and waited for the conversation to move on.

Sergeant Travers opened his notebook and asked some preliminary questions before the detective turned to the murder.

'Can you tell me when you last saw Lady Chichester?' he asked.

'I saw her in the maze,' said Lottie. 'About five minutes before she was attacked. I was lost, and she told me the way out.'

'Five minutes before she was attacked, you say?'

Lottie nodded.

'We've established the attack took place just after half-past eight this evening. So you saw her just before half-past, you think?'

Lottie nodded again.

'And when you saw her, was there anyone else about?'

'There were other people in the maze, but I didn't see anyone else when I spoke to her.'

'Did you see anyone who could have been following her after you went on your way?'

'No.'

He drew in a sharp breath. 'This is what puzzles me, you see. For someone to attack her in a maze, they must have been following her to know her exact position. And once they'd determined her position, they managed to position themselves on the opposite side of the hedge. It's no mean feat.'

'Especially in that maze,' said Mrs Moore. 'It's so easy to lose your bearings and get lost.'

'Indeed. The only way to successfully track someone down in there is to follow them.'

'Maybe the attacker just got lucky,' said Mrs Moore.

'That's a possibility, I suppose. But this attack was planned. The assailant went into that maze armed with a knife. I can't imagine he or she was merely hoping they'd get lucky. How well did you know Lady Chichester, Mrs Moore?'

'Not very well at all, Detective. I've known Lord Chichester for a few years, but this weekend was the first time I'd met her.'

'Can you think of anyone who wished to harm her?'

'Not really. Apart from the strange fact she threatened to tell people that Quentin Lawrence's mother wrote his songs. Maybe Mr Lawrence wished to silence her about that. But he saw her regularly, so why wait until she was in a maze to murder her?'

'Confusion,' said Lottie.

'Yes!' The detective pointed his pen at her again. 'That could be why. Everyone was running about in that maze hopelessly lost and he took advantage of the chaos.'

'And there's Miss Darby,' said Mrs Moore. 'She had quite a moan to me and Miss Sprigg about Lady Chichester. She felt she received favourable treatment from Mr Lawrence and she told us there were plans to make the Pom-Pom Duo a trio with Lady Chichester as the main star.'

'An accusation has been levelled that Miss Darby was jealous of Lady Chichester? Do you think that's correct?'

'I think there could be something in it. Although I can't imagine Miss Darby being a murderess.'

'Interesting. Have you written all this down, Travers?' The sergeant nodded.

'And I've just thought of someone else,' said Mrs Moore. 'I don't like to suggest this person because I like her and I know she's had a difficult few years. But I'm afraid it's Lady Forbes-Chichester.'

'The first Lady Chichester?'

'Yes. She interrupted Lady Chichester's performance and all the guests were asked to go outside while she was removed from the ballroom. That's when everyone went into the maze and got lost.'

'So she created the chaos?'

'Yes. If she hadn't disrupted the performance, no one would have ended up in the maze.'

'Did you see her in the maze?'

'No.'

'Do you know what happened to her after she disrupted the performance?'

'No, I think the footmen escorted her out of the house.'

'So she couldn't have got into the maze to attack Lady Chichester?'

'I don't know. I suppose she could have done. There were so many people about that maybe she managed to sneak in as part of the crowd.'

LORD CHICHESTER SAT opposite the detective and the police sergeant with a large glass of brandy in his hand.

'Was your marriage a happy one, Lord Chichester?'

'Now that's not a nice question to be asking a chap who's just lost his wife. But I'll forgive you for it, Detective, because I know you've got a job to do. And I want you to do it well. I want this man caught!'

'Very good, my lord. So, do you have an answer to my question?'

'Oh yes. Our marriage was very happy indeed.' He looked Detective Inspector Wilson in the eye to show how sincere he was.

'You weren't married for long.'

'No. We were celebrating our first wedding anniversary this very weekend.' He blinked away the dampness in his eyes.

'And when did you last see your wife?'

'Well, we'd just dealt with an incident. A disruptive guest, in fact. Actually, she wasn't a guest. She invited herself. We saw her out of the door and told the staff to get the room ready for the evening's dancing. Ruby and I went out onto the terrace to find our guests and discovered they'd all run off into the maze. We couldn't quite believe it, they were behaving like a pack of unruly children! A few had got themselves out of it again, but I know how long it can take some people. It's the largest maze in England! Ruby and I were keen to get on with the dances because the band were only booked until eleven. We didn't want to start late and lose out. So we went into the maze to help everyone get out again. I went right, and she went left.' He felt his voice choke, and he paused.

'That's when you last saw her?' said the detective.

'Yes. That was the last time.' He put his brandy down, pulled his handkerchief out of his pocket and dabbed at his eyes.

'You didn't see her again while you were in the maze trying to round everyone up?'

'No. That was the last time. I just wish I could have said something else to her, like a proper farewell. Instead, I said something like "You go that way, and I'll go this way" and that was that.'

'Were you in the maze at the time of the murder?'

'Yes, I was. And I thought it was someone playing a joke for a moment. Then I realised it was serious. A terrible hulla-baloo. You need to speak to everyone who was in that maze at the time. Someone must have seen something.'

'I will speak to them all.'

'You need to find holes in Miss Darby's statement. I think she did it, you know. She has this story about a knife being poked through the hedge, but it doesn't wash with me. It's obviously her and I don't understand why you haven't arrested her yet.'

'We're extremely interested in what Miss Darby has to say for herself, but we need a little more evidence before we can arrest her. What would Miss Darby's motive be for murdering your wife, do you think?'

'She was jealous of her. Everyone's been saying it, Detective. It's quite obvious. She wanted a bigger role for herself in the duo.'

'But your wife's tragic death has put an end to the duo. Murdering her would be self-defeating for Miss Darby.'

'Yes. But perhaps she's not very clever and didn't think it through properly. There's no doubt she's behind this. And she's trying to explain it with the arm through the hedge nonsense.'

'You say you didn't see your wife in the maze, Lord Chichester. But you may have heard her voice through a hedge?'

'No, I didn't.'

'So while the two ladies held their brief conversation, you didn't pass by on the other side of the hedge and hear them talking?'

'No. I was too busy looking for people who were lost and needed help to get out of there. I didn't hear their conversation. And we only have Miss Darby's word that the conversation took place. For all we know, she crept up on my wife and did the act.'

'I'm inclined to believe Miss Darby because she said your wife brought up a disagreement which she'd had with Mr Lawrence. Mr Lawrence has confirmed the disagreement took place, and it was overheard by Miss Sprigg, too.'

'Fair point. Perhaps my wife mentioned the disagreement to Miss Darby before they went into the maze? Miss Darby could be bending the truth.'

'How is your relationship with your first wife, Lord Chichester?'

Anna. Why did he have to talk about her, too? He didn't like discussing personal matters, but the detective was likely to interpret any reluctance to talk as guilt.

'We get on well for the sake of the children.'

'How many children do you have?'

'Four sons and one daughter. They're all grown up and doing well for themselves.'

'Good. It's always nice when children do well for themselves, isn't it? I have reason to believe the uninvited guest you mentioned earlier was your first wife.'

'Yes.'

'Why did she turn up uninvited?'

'To cause trouble, I think.'

'Do you know why?'

'She didn't like Ruby. Which is understandable because Ruby ended our marriage.'

'Were you not also responsible for it ending?'

'I suppose I had a part in it too, yes.'

'So your first wife, Lady Forbes-Chichester, turned up at the party and interrupted your second wife's performance.'

'Yes.'

'There's been a suggestion your first wife could be the murderer.'

Lord Chichester felt his mouth drop open. 'Who's suggested that?'

'I shall keep the source anonymous for the time being.'

'Anonymous, eh? Too cowardly to suggest it to my face! You can tell the anonymous source from me that their suggestion is a load of utter codswallop.'

'So you don't believe your first wife is capable of such a thing?'

'Never!'

'But her disruption of your wife's performance this evening suggests a desire for revenge.'

'It wasn't behaviour befitting of a lady, I admit that. Everyone knows Lady Forbes-Chichester and I have had our differences in recent years. But I will defend that lady to the hilt. I can't deny she was angry about the affair. It was a torrid time for us all. But my dear first wife does not have an evil bone in her entire body.'

'But she turned up at your wedding anniversary party and booed your wife's performance.'

'It wasn't her finest hour. She may have booed Ruby's performance, but she certainly would never have murdered her. It's absolutely impossible. In fact, the thought of it makes me quite upset.' He dabbed his eyes again.

'Purely for argument's sake,' said the detective. 'Can you tell me if it's possible your former wife could have entered the maze with no one noticing?'

'No. And she simply wouldn't have done it. She would have felt rather ashamed of herself after being rude to my wife, and she would have left.'

'Very well. I think a conversation with Lady Forbes-Chichester should clear this up.'

'I'm sure it will.'

Lord Chichester couldn't help leaping to his first wife's defence. The truth was, he still loved her. If only he could admit to the detective that he wished he'd never been unfaithful to her. But she'd divorced him and he'd remarried without a thought. It had all happened so quickly.

He had made a mistake. A very big one. But it would be shameful to admit to anyone that he regretted his decisions.

Chapter Twenty-Three

LOTTIE AND MRS MOORE sat with Mrs Stanley-Piggot at breakfast the following morning. Out of respect for Lady Chichester, they wore dark, subdued clothes and talked in hushed tones. Mr and Mrs Lawrence sat at a table nearby, as did Miss Darby. There was no sign of Lord Chichester.

'The detective has asked to speak to me this morning,' said Mrs Stanley-Piggot. 'I don't know why. I can't help him, can I?'

'Can you not?'

'No. I didn't know Lady Chichester very well. I know the first Lady Chichester well and I think it's an enormous shame that... oh, never mind.'

'That the marriage ended?'

'Yes. Dreadful. Anyway, I know William extremely well, of course. He and my late husband, Francis, were good friends.'

'How did they meet?'

'It was shortly after William inherited this place. He returned from the second Boer War and found himself saddled with a country estate from his great uncle. He didn't know many people in polite society, so he wrote to all the landed gentry in the area and invited them to Hamilton Hall. From that moment onwards, he and Francis were firm friends. My husband inherited the family business and a large fortune, so he was able to give him some good advice.'

'How long were you married for?'

'Thirty-three years, four months and seventeen days.'

'Golly, that's precise.'

'We were blissfully happy.'

'That's lovely to hear.'

'We never exchanged a cross word in all that time.'

'I'm impressed. How did your husband's family make their fortune?'

'Biscuits.'

'Biscuits? Yummy.'

'Francis never liked biscuits, so he sold the company to a large food manufacturer. They gave him a very good price for it.'

Lottie recalled Lord Chichester saying Mrs Stanley-Piggot was one of the richest widows in the country.

'I was born into money too,' said Mrs Stanley-Piggot. 'My father was Lord Stanley-Piggot and my mother was a Lyon-Arkwright.'

'The Lyon-Arkwrights? Very well known.'

'They are. You seem quite knowledgeable about English society, Mrs Moore. For an American.'

'Yes, I make it my business to find out what I can.'

'Good for you. It's important to do so when you're moving in these circles. It's a shame the pair of us haven't met sooner.'

'Yes, it is rather, isn't it?'

'We must arrange to meet when everything has calmed down again.'

'I would like that. You're welcome to visit me in Chelsea at any time which suits.'

'I have a house in Chelsea too! So now we have no excuse for not seeing each other in the future. Although I'm quite busy these days making my investments. Along with Nelson's Column, I have also invested in an art collection.'

'Have you indeed?'

'Yes, I'm very proud of it. My most recent purchase is The Hay Wain by John Constable.'

'That famous picture of a cart stuck in a river?'

'Yes. Is it stuck? I thought the horses were pulling it across the river.'

'Maybe they are, then. Did you buy it at auction?'

'No. I bought it through a broker.'

'Mr Jones who sold you Nelson's Column?'

'No, this is a very nice chap called Mr King. But the two know each other.'

'The Hay Wain is a very popular picture. You must have some security to keep it at your home.'

'It's not in my home. It was a condition of its sale that it remains in the National Gallery.'

'So the National Gallery sold it to you, but said the picture should remain there?'

'Yes. I like to visit the picture every few weeks and admire it.'

'Can you be sure you actually own it?'

'Of course! I have all the paperwork. Reams of the stuff. So if anybody needs any proof of ownership, I have it.'

'That's good then.'

Mrs Moore gave Lottie a sidelong glance and Lottie knew what she was thinking. It seemed Mrs Stanley-Piggot had fallen prey to another confidence trickster.

Mrs Moore clearly decided not to raise the matter now

and changed the subject instead. 'Well, I hope all goes well in your interview with Detective Inspector Wilson. You say you won't be able to help him, but you might be surprised. Even the smallest observation could be a crucial clue.'

'I doubt it in my case. It will just be a waste of his time.'

MARGARET STANLEY-PIGGOT MADE her way to the morning room where Detective Inspector Wilson and a police officer were waiting for her. The sight of them made her feel like she'd done something wrong.

'I've just been telling the American lady that I won't be able to help you,' she said as she sat in one of the comfortable chairs. 'I didn't hear or see anything suspicious.'

'In which case, our chat will probably be quick, Mrs Stanley-Piggot. But it's important we speak to everyone.'

'Of course.'

The sergeant opened his notebook and readied himself with a pen.

'How do you know Lord Chichester?' asked the detective.

'He was an old friend of my late husband, Francis.' Margaret explained the history of their friendship, just as she had told it to Mrs Moore and her young companion.

'And you're a widow now.'

'Yes, my dear husband died last year. William has kindly invited me here a couple of times since my husband's death. He's been very kind to me.'

'And how well did you know Lady Chichester?'

'Not very well. I knew the first Lady Chichester very well, and we were good friends. I only met the second Lady Chichester a few times. We didn't have a great deal in common.'

'What was your relationship with her like?'

'I wouldn't describe it as a relationship. We were acquaintances who were polite and friendly with one another.'

'Can you think of anyone who would want to harm her?'

'No. But what would I know? I barely knew her.'

'You say you were good friends with the first Lady Chichester. Is it possible you bore some resentment towards the second Lady Chichester?'

'No.'

The swiftness of her answer made the detective raise an eyebrow. 'Are you sure?' he said.

Margaret sighed. He had caught her out. Would it matter if she told him the truth?

She took in a breath and decided to be honest. 'I thought it was a terrible shame when William had an affair with Ruby Higgins. He threw away years of happy marriage.'

William had been a fool. And everyone knew Ruby Higgins was the sort who threw herself at men with wealth and status. Margaret had no time for women like that. She felt sure Ruby had never loved William, but she didn't want to appear too vindictive. Instead, she tried to speak tactfully. 'Lady Chichester seemed a nice young woman, but there was no need for her to end William's marriage like that. She should have found someone her own age.'

She hadn't liked the second Lady Chichester. But Miss Darby was far worse.

'You disapproved of Lord Chichester's second marriage?' asked the detective.

'No,' she lied. 'I was just surprised by it. However, William was free to make whatever decisions he wished to. If he hadn't met Ruby, then he would still be married to Anna, his first wife. But it's none of my business, Detective. Whatever opinions or feelings I may have about the matter, they're not important. And I don't see why you need to be asking me about them.'

'Anything that causes friction and conflict interests us, Mrs Stanley-Piggot. Someone who murders is not a happy and content person. They are perhaps bitter, out for revenge, or seeking to remove someone for their own gain. I realise it's not pleasant dwelling on these things, but these are the reasons why people commit murder.'

'If you think Lady Chichester was murdered because she put an end to William's first marriage, then I say you're mistaken.'

'The first Lady Chichester turned up uninvited yesterday evening and interrupted the second Lady Chichester's performance.'

'Yes, she did. But that doesn't make her a murderer! She's clearly still upset about the divorce. And who can blame her? If it had been me, I would have been furious! Even a few years after the event. That sort of anger doesn't go away overnight, you know. However, Anna would never have harmed the second Lady Chichester. Being rude to her was enough, I think.'

'Interesting.' The detective turned to the sergeant. 'Have you made a note of all this, Travers?'

'Yes, sir.'

'And your handwriting is legible this time?'

'Indeed it is, sir.'

'Good.' Detective Inspector Wilson turned back to Margaret. Her head was aching with all the concentration.

'Will this take much longer?' she asked.

'No, not much longer.'

'Your time really would be better spent questioning other people.'

'Very well. Just a few more questions. When did you last see Lady Chichester?'

'When she performed that song about falling in love with a sailor.'

'You didn't see her after that?'

'No.'

'You didn't bump into her in the maze?'

'No.'

'Were you in the maze at the time of the murder?'

'Yes I was. The scream frightened the absolute living daylights out of me! And as soon as I heard the word "murder" I tried to get out of there as quickly as I could. Terrifying.'

'You didn't try to help?'

'No! What could I do? And with the knowledge there was a murderer lurking in that maze, I was desperate to get out of there in one piece.' She shuddered at the memory. 'And luckily I did.'

LOTTIE TOOK Rosie for a walk in the garden. It was a beautiful spring morning, and the birds were singing a happy morning chorus. The sun had some warmth in it and there was a pleasant scent from the spring flowers. They strolled along the terrace and Lottie eyed the maze. She recalled the detective saying there was only one way in and out of the maze, but was it possible to squeeze through a gap somewhere?

If it was possible, then it could have helped the murderer carry out the attack undetected.

'Come along, Rosie,' she said. 'Let's walk around the perimeter of the maze. We need to look for gaps. You check the bottom of the hedge, and I'll look at the rest of it.'

The perimeter hedge was tall, thick, and neatly clipped. Lottie could tell from its little needle green leaves it was yew. A narrow gravel path followed the perimeter and Lottie and Rosie walked along it, looking for gaps.

They completed one side of the maze, turned left, and began to walk along the next length. On their right, the extensive grounds of Hamilton Hall sloped downhill to the river. It

78

was easy to see why Ruby Higgins had been so keen to marry Lord Chichester and live in this beautiful place.

They had almost reached the next corner when Rosie stopped and pushed her nose into the hedge.

'Have you found a gap?' Lottie stooped down to have a look. There was a gap at the foot of the hedge which was large enough for a hedgehog, rabbit or small cat to push through. But as Lottie looked more closely, she realised this part of the hedge was quite thin. There was a wider-than-usual gap between two yew shrubs. Lottie pushed her arm between the branches and could see this part of the hedge was thin enough to push her way through.

'It's not really a gap,' she said to Rosie. 'But I think someone could get through here if they really wanted to.'

Something colourful caught her eye. A tiny piece of fabric snagged on a twig.

'Someone has pushed their way through here!' she said. She reached out, pulled the little piece of fabric off the twig and dropped it into the palm of her hand.

Her heart thudded as she stared at it.

In the centre of her palm lay a tiny piece of plum-purple satin.

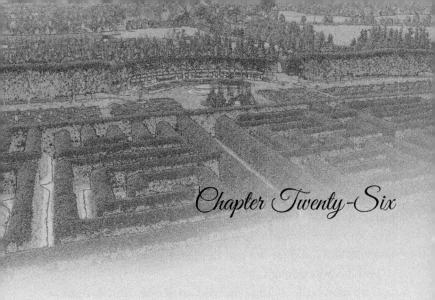

Chapter Twenty-Six

'IT's important that we understand exactly what happened,' said Detective Inspector Wilson. 'Can you tell me again about the attack on Lady Chichester.'

Daisy Darby sighed. 'But I've already told you about it, Detective! And it was so horrible.'

'I realise this isn't easy for you, Miss Darby. But perhaps you might recall a detail which you previously forgot? Sergeant Travers here will write down everything you say to ensure we have a proper record. And you're going to use your best handwriting, aren't you, Travers?'

'I'll do my best, sir. Although I have to write quickly to keep up.'

'Please do your best not to sacrifice quality for the sake of speed.'

Daisy took out a cigarette from the packet in her handbag. 'Do you mind if I smoke, Detective?'

'Not at all. If it helps you remember every tiny bit of detail, then all the better.'

She felt calmer once she'd inhaled on her cigarette. 'Can

this please be the last time I explain it all? I don't like reliving it over and over.'

'I can't promise that, Miss Darby. After all, once we've collared the suspect, it's likely you'll have to give evidence in court at the trial.'

'I have to go to court?' A shudder ran through her spine. 'I don't think I could bear it!'

'You're a performer, Miss Darby. Surely the witness stand isn't too different to the stage?'

'They're completely different! One is fun and I get paid for it. But standing up in court? I hate the idea!'

'Let's forget I mentioned it.' He scratched his temple. 'A trial only occurs once we've charged a suspect. And we're not making much progress with that at the moment. Now tell us what happened after you went into the maze yesterday evening, Miss Darby.'

'I got lost.'

'And who did you see in there?'

'Lots of people!'

'Did you see Lord Chichester?'

'No.' She named the guests she'd known the names of. 'And then I bumped into Ruby, which I was very relieved about because she said she'd tell me how to get out again.'

'And you had a conversation, didn't you?'

'Yes.' She repeated the story Ruby had told her about Mr Lawrence complaining about her performance. He had always been so picky with Ruby because she'd been his favourite. Sometimes Daisy had wished he'd been as particular about her performances. Indifference sometimes felt worse than criticism. But Ruby had been more bothered than usual by it, and that had been because she'd wanted to enjoy her anniversary celebrations without Quentin Lawrence breathing down her neck.

'Were you still discussing Mr Lawrence at the time of the attack?' asked the detective.

'Yes. I was saying something sympathetic to her. I can't remember my exact words, but it was something like "that was uncalled for, especially in your own home" and then she gave me an odd stare. I asked her if she was alright and she gasped and fell to the ground. That's when I saw the knife in her lower back. And I screamed without thinking and cried out "murder" because it so obviously was!'

Daisy shook her head in dismay and inhaled deeply on her cigarette.

'And to be clear, you didn't see the hand holding the knife?'

'No. Ruby was standing in the way.'

'So you don't know if the hand belonged to a man or a woman?'

'No.'

'You didn't see anything on the other side of the hedge?'

'No. It was too thick.'

'Did you hear anything?'

'No. And the moment I saw that odd, glazed expression on Ruby's face, I was completely distracted. I was trying to find out what was wrong with her and giving no thought to who was beyond the hedge. Have you found any fingerprints on the knife?'

'Unfortunately not. We're quite certain the assailant must have been wearing gloves.'

'Well, all the ladies were wearing evening gloves. And I suppose a man could have carried a pair of gloves in his pocket. If he'd planned to carry a knife to murder Lady Chichester, then he must have planned to carry gloves, too.'

'What was your relationship with Ruby like?'

'We were very good friends. We first met in a dance troupe five years ago.'

'Did your friendship change after her marriage to Lord Chichester?'

'A little bit.'

'In what way?'

'She became the more important one. Look, I know everyone says I was jealous of her, but I wasn't.'

'Are you seeking a title of your own?'

'What do you mean by that?'

'There are rumours of a liaison with Lord Moorcroft.'

Daisy's stomach gave a flip. 'How did you hear those rumours?'

'Is there truth in them?' His eyes narrowed.

'I don't see what this has got to do with Ruby's murder! Lord Moorcroft has seen some of our performances and visited backstage. That is all.'

'Perhaps you wish to emulate Lady Chichester's success and have a house like this one day?'

'No. I have no interest in that.'

'Really? That's surprising. I think many people would like a house like this. And what about being the star of the show?'

'What do you mean?'

'Is that what you want?'

'I want to be successful, yes. But if you're suggesting I murdered Ruby to further my own ambition, then you're completely wrong, Detective! How could I possibly be that cold-hearted?'

She took a final drag on her cigarette and squashed it angrily into the cut glass ashtray.

Why did everyone assume she was envious of Ruby and wanted her out of the way? Her death had put an end to the Pom-Pom Duo. And where did that leave Daisy now?

Ruby's death had also put an end to the plans for the Pom-Pom Trio. And Daisy felt some relief about that. And with the Pom-Pom Duo gone, her contract was surely irrelevant too. With a bit of luck, she was free to follow her own path now.

Chapter Twenty-Seven

LOTTIE WALKED with Rosie back to the house with the small piece of plum-purple satin tucked into the pocket of her skirt.

Could it really have come from Mrs Moore's dress? She tried to recall how many other ladies had been wearing purple the previous evening. There had been a large lady in lilac and a grey-haired lady in violet, but their dresses had been different shades of purple.

She pictured again the moment she'd seen Mrs Moore after they'd both escaped from the maze. Her employer had been limping wearily along the terrace in her enormous plum-purple gown. She hadn't mentioned that she'd squeezed through a gap in the hedge. Why had she kept it secret?

The gap in the hedge could have provided the perfect escape route for a murderer keen to flee the scene of their crime.

Lottie felt nauseous. Surely Mrs Moore wasn't hiding something? She hoped she was mistaken and that the piece of plum-purple satin had come from another dress. There was only one way to check, and that was to examine the gown Mrs Moore had worn the previous evening.

On their return to the house, Lottie and Rosie encountered Mrs Moore in the entrance hall. Lady Chichester stared down at them from her oversized portrait.

'Oh, there you are, Lottie! Did you have a nice walk? Coffee is being served in the sitting room. Come and join me.'

Now that she faced Mrs Moore, Lottie didn't know what to say. Should she tell her about the piece of fabric she'd found and gauge her reaction? Or should she check the gown first?

There were a few guests being served coffee in the sitting room, and Lottie noticed Sally the maid. The pair exchanged a smile.

As they made themselves comfortable in some easy chairs, Lottie tried to reassure herself that Mrs Moore couldn't possibly be a murderer.

'Are you alright, Lottie?' said Mrs Moore. 'You're rather quiet and you have an odd expression on your face.'

'Am I? Do I?' A hot flush washed over her. Lottie knew she was hopeless at lying or hiding anything. 'I'm a little bit tired,' she added. 'I didn't sleep very well.'

This explanation seemed to satisfy Mrs Moore. 'Yes, it's not surprising. Oh, good morning, Miss Darby.'

'Do you mind if I join you?' The blonde-haired young woman sank into an easy chair next to Mrs Moore. She wore a black dress and scarlet red lipstick. 'I've just had to speak to Detective Inspector Wilson again. The police don't make it easy for you, do they?'

'No, I suppose it's his job to put us on the spot.'

'I just wish I hadn't been there when it happened because everyone assumes I did it! Do you mind if I smoke?'

'No. It sounds like you need to.'

'I do!' She lit her cigarette, then blew out a ring of smoke. 'The detective is wasting his time with the wrong people,' she said.

'Who do you think he should speak to then?' said Mrs Moore.

Miss Darby glanced over both shoulders before leaning forward and lowering her voice. 'I don't think Maria Lawrence was particularly impressed when her husband took us under his wing.'

'Why not?'

'Because she's a snob. She looks down on performers like me and Ruby. I think she also felt envious about the amount of attention her husband was giving to Ruby. It was only professional attention. Nothing untoward ever happened between them, so Mrs Lawrence needn't have worried. But I don't think that was her main concern, anyway. I think she thought he was wasting his time with us and that there were worthier people to work with instead. But we earned quite a bit of money for him, so she was stuck with us.'

'Interesting,' said Mrs Moore. 'And how did Maria Lawrence and Lady Chichester get on with each other?'

'Fortunately, we didn't see her very often. But sometimes Mr Lawrence invited us to their house to discuss a performance or our plans. If Mrs Lawrence was there too, then the atmosphere was frosty.' She lowered her voice even more. 'And the trouble with Mrs Lawrence is she thinks she knows best. She may be a Shakespearean actress, but she thinks she knows the job of a popular performer, too. And she doesn't at all. So when we were discussing something, she couldn't resist chipping in with ideas of her own. And they were quite silly ideas, of course. I tried to bite my lip and not say too much about it. But Ruby couldn't help herself, she would disagree with her there and then. It could become quite uncomfortable and awkward at times.'

'Have you told the detective this?'

Miss Darby sat back in her chair. 'No. It will only make me sound like I'm the guilty person trying to put the blame on someone else. He's already suspicious of me as it is. If he's a good enough detective, then he'll find out all this for himself, won't he? The Lawrences will tell him. If they're honest, that is.'

'You think they might lie?'

Miss Darby shrugged. 'Who knows? If they've got something to hide, then I'm sure they will.'

The conversation then turned to theatre, and Lottie made an excuse to leave. 'I'd like to fetch my book from my room,' she said.

'Of course, Lottie,' said Mrs Moore. 'I'll see you shortly.'

ROSIE ACCOMPANIED Lottie as she fetched her book from her room. Once she had it in her hand, she closed her door and stood in the quiet corridor. There was no one else around.

The door to Mrs Moore's room was next to them.

'Now's my opportunity,' she whispered to Rosie. 'It will only take me a minute to check her gown.'

She turned the handle of the door and stepped into the pink, rose-themed room. Once Rosie was inside too, Lottie hurriedly closed the door and dashed over to the shiny walnut wardrobe in the corner. She flung open the doors, and the gown was hanging in front of her.

Lottie pulled out the piece of fabric from her pocket and compared it to the gown. It was an identical match.

'But someone else could have worn a dress with the same fabric, don't you think, Rosie?'

The corgi looked up at her with large, dark eyes.

It was dingy in the wardrobe, and the dress had yards of fabric in its skirt. Lottie took it out of the wardrobe and laid it on the bed so she could inspect it more closely. She knew this was risky. Mrs Moore could return at any moment. But she could see a lot better with the light from the window. Her palms felt damp as she hurriedly sifted through the fabric. As she failed to find a hole, her hopes rose that she'd been mistaken all along.

'I can't find anything, Rosie. It must have come from someone else's dress.'

But just as she spoke, Lottie found the small tear she'd been looking for. It was the same size as the piece of missing fabric.

She stared at it for a moment. What did it mean?

Then she had no time to think as the handle of the door began to turn.

In an instant, Lottie returned the dress to the wardrobe. She was just closing the doors when Mrs Moore stepped in.

Chapter Twenty-Nine

'Lottie?' Mrs Moore stared at her.

Lottie opened her mouth and closed it again, unsure of what to say.

'Are you looking for something?'

Lottie nodded and held out the tiny piece of fabric. 'I found this snagged on a twig in a hedge in the maze this morning. It looks like it's from your gown.'

Mrs Moore stepped forward and took it from her. 'Yes, I believe it is. I must have caught my dress somewhere.' Then she gave Lottie a suspicious glance. 'I thought you were in an odd mood earlier, Lottie. What's going on?'

Lottie told her about the gap in the hedge. 'And I was so sure the piece of fabric came from your dress that I came in here to check.'

'Why didn't you ask me about it?'

'I don't know.' She couldn't bring herself to tell Mrs Moore she suspected the murderer had fled through the gap.

'You could have just asked me, Lottie. I would have told you it was from my dress.'

'But that means you went through the gap.'

'Yes, I did. That's how I got out of the maze, Lottie! I couldn't bear being in there for a moment longer. I'd lost you and I'd lost the grey-whiskered man I was trying to follow. I was fed up and dizzy from going round and round trying to find my way out. I came across a part of the hedge which looked a bit thinner than the rest and decided to push through it. I'm not proud of myself because I don't think it did the hedge a great deal of good. I felt my dress catch as I went through, I didn't realise I tore it and I'm rather annoyed about that. Hopefully, I can find someone who'll repair it for me. You could have asked me this, Lottie. Why were you so secretive?'

Lottie gave a relieved laugh. 'It was because you didn't mention it to me, I thought you might be hiding something.'

'I was going to tell you what I'd done when we met on the terrace, but then the scream interrupted us.'

'Oh yes.' The memory of that scream gave Lottie a cold shiver.

'I forgot to mention it after that,' said Mrs Moore.

'And I got the idea into my head that the only person who would have squeezed their way through the hedge would have been the murderer,' said Lottie. 'They must have known about the gap and pushed their way out without being seen.'

'So when you saw the piece of fabric, you assumed I was the murderer, Lottie?'

'Not really...'

'But you did!' A smile spread across Mrs Moore's face. 'Oh, Lottie! The fact you're even willing to suspect me shows how seriously you take your investigations! I can picture you now sipping your coffee and considering different reasons why I would want to murder Lady Chichester!'

'I suppose I was a little bit. It's very silly of me.'

Mrs Moore laughed. 'I can see why you were suspicious. And you could be right about something. The murderer may well have taken that route in or out of the maze and they managed to do so without leaving behind a small piece of their clothing.'

'I'd like to find out how close that gap in the hedge is to the scene of the murder,' said Lottie. 'If the two locations are close, then that could be why the murderer has escaped detection.'

'I don't know how you can find out without going into the maze again.'

'I could go in there with a ball of string. Like Theseus did when he went into the labyrinth.'

'Who?'

'It's a Greek myth.'

'Oh.'

'Theseus killed the minotaur.'

'Oh yes, I recall it now. Well, there was certainly a minotaur in the maze last night. Very unpleasant. If you must go back to the maze again, Lottie, then be careful. The murderer is still at large.'

'But they won't still be in the maze.'

'How do we know where they are? Just be careful, Lottie.'

Chapter Thirty

DETECTIVE INSPECTOR WILSON'S jacket was too small for him. It was tight around the shoulders and Quentin Lawrence felt sure it was unlikely to fasten comfortably at the front. The detective wore it unbuttoned over a waistcoat which wasn't an exact match of navy blue. It had probably been bought separately to the jacket. The waistcoat fitted alright, so it was probably a replacement for the original one which had matched the jacket. The detective's shirt collar was a little uneven too, it was probably quite cheap. Quentin was tempted to march the detective to his tailor once this interview was over and done with.

'How long did you work with Lady Chichester for, Mr Lawrence?'

'Two years.'

'And how well did you know her?'

'Extremely well. She was like a sister to me.'

'How did you meet?'

'I saw her in a show at the Hackney Empire and I thought she was simply wonderful. She was the shining light on the stage. So I spoke to her backstage and told her she must simply sing my songs. That was that.'

'She was performing in the Pom-Pom Duo at the time?'

'Yes, I had to take on the pair of them. Ruby insisted on it. I was reluctant at first, but Daisy got better. In fact, she's not too bad at all these days.'

'But you preferred Lady Chichester?'

'Yes! Who wouldn't? As a performer, she had that quality which is impossible to describe. That *je ne sais quoi*, as the French put it.'

'How do you spell that?' asked the police sergeant who was making notes.

'Don't worry about that bit, Travers,' said Detective Inspector Wilson.

'But you told me to write down everything, sir.'

'Yes, but the gist of that will be fine.' The detective turned back to Quentin. 'How was your working relationship with Lady Chichester?'

'Simply perfect. In fact, she was the inspiration for many of my songs. I don't know how I'm going to write another one after this. I feel like all creativity has left me now.'

'She seemed quite upset about your criticism of her performance.'

Quentin waved this question away. 'It was normal.'

'You normally spoke to her like that?'

'Yes! And she'd get upset about it and then threaten me with something-or-other.'

'Threaten you with what?'

'Oh... for example, telling people that my mother wrote my songs. That was typical of Ruby. We fell out all the time. And then we made up again. That's how it worked. It's like that in show business, Detective. You need sparks! Sometimes you even need fire. Sometimes everything has to be completely burned and destroyed in order for something new to grow through the ashes. It's what I call the creative cycle.'

The detective's eyes narrowed. The poor man didn't understand because he didn't have a creative bone in his body. Nor did he have a decent tailor.

'Can you think of anyone who wished to harm Lady Chichester?'

'No one.'

'Are you sure about that? I remember reading about the Chichester divorce in the papers. Ruby Higgins, as she was called then, was accused of wrecking the family.'

'Well, that's the papers for you, Detective.'

'And some people have mentioned Miss Darby was jealous of Lady Chichester.'

'Jealousy is quite normal in show business. It's a competitive world. And besides, you need jealousy in our industry.'

'It's part of the creative cycle?'

'Very good, Detective. I wasn't quite going to say that. I was going to say it keeps everyone on their toes.'

'Were there any disagreements between Miss Darby and Lady Chichester?'

'Other than a little silly bickering, no.'

'Did Lady Chichester mention she was worried about anything?'

'No. She had some nerves about performing yesterday but you need nerves in order to perform. If you don't have nerves, it means you don't care about what you're doing.'

'So you have no idea who harmed her?'

'None whatsoever!' He gave the detective a smile. 'Are we finished?'

Detective Inspector Wilson gave a nod.

As Quentin got up to leave, he felt a shiver. Ruby's words repeated in his mind.

If your career came to an end, Quentin, you would mind very much, wouldn't you?

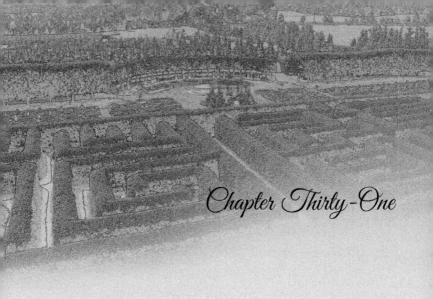

Chapter Thirty-One

LORD CHICHESTER SAT in the sitting room that afternoon, looking mournful. There were dark circles beneath his eyes, and his grey hair was unkempt.

'Would you like to join Miss Sprigg and me for a walk, Lord Chichester?' asked Mrs Moore. 'You look like you could do with some fresh air.'

'That's very kind of you, Mrs Moore, but I'm alright here.'

'Are you sure?'

'Yes. I want to have a word with the detective once he's finished speaking to Mr Lawrence.' He sighed. 'I don't understand all this. I keep expecting Ruby to walk into the room at any moment.'

'I can imagine, Lord Chichester. These tragedies can take a while to sink in.'

'They certainly can.' He rubbed his brow. 'But I can suggest a pleasant walk for you, Mrs Moore.'

'Oh, don't trouble yourself with suggesting one at a time like this, Lord Chichester.'

'No, I insist. I welcome the distraction. There's a lovely walk by the river which is about a mile. Is that long enough?'

'Easily long enough.'

'Good. It's a charming route which Ruby and I used to... anyway. Start by walking down the driveway until you reach a little group of workers' cottages. Turn right there and you'll see a path forking to your left. Follow that for fifty yards and you'll reach the river. Turn right onto the riverside path and it will bring you all the way along to the back of the house. Or you can do the walk in reverse. Either way, it's a lovely stroll.'

'Thank you, Lord Chichester.'

He turned to Lottie. 'Did you bring your sketchbook with you, young lady?'

Lottie wondered why all gentlemen of a certain age assumed young women had sketchbooks.

'Not this time,' she said.

'Pity. Although if you have a look in the drawers in the morning room, I think Ruby had a few sketchbooks which...'

'Thank you, Lord Chichester,' said Mrs Moore as his face grew more wretched. 'We'll be on our way.'

'Poor Lord Chichester,' said Mrs Moore as she, Lottie and Rosie began their walk down the driveway. 'He's still in complete shock, isn't he? And I expect he's under suspicion, too. The police often consider the husband in these sorts of cases, don't they?'

'He was in the maze when Lady Chichester was murdered,' said Lottie.

'He was indeed. Perhaps he has an alibi for the time of her murder. Who knows? Hopefully, Detective Inspector Wilson will apprehend someone soon. He seems competent enough. Oh look, here are the workers' cottages.' She peered through her lorgnette at a row of little red brick homes. 'Lord Chichester said we turn right here then... where next?'

'We'll see a path forking to our left.'

'I'm glad you remember these things, Lottie.'

As they turned right, a stooped old lady in a shawl and headscarf watched them from her gate.

'Good afternoon!' Mrs Moore called out to her. 'We're off for a stroll along the river. Are we heading the right way?'

The old lady stared at them but said nothing.

'Maybe she's deaf,' whispered Mrs Moore to Lottie. 'She could at least wave to us though, couldn't she? She looks a little odd, actually.'

The old lady opened her gate, stepped through it and hobbled towards them.

'It looks like she prefers to conduct her conversation close up, Lottie.' They waited as she hobbled closer. Her face was heavily lined, and she had large pale blue eyes. Her lips were pushed into a downward pout.

She stopped in front of Mrs Moore. She was about a foot shorter than her and had to twist her neck and head up to look at her.

'Good afternoon!' said Mrs Moore again.

'Naughty Tommy,' said the old lady.

'Naughty Tommy?' Mrs Moore gave Lottie a sidelong glance. 'Who's he?'

The old lady pointed at Hamilton Hall. 'Naughty Tommy. He stole from his lordship.'

'Did he now? Well, that is naughty then. What did he steal?'

The old lady stared at them both, then looked down at Rosie and patted her on the head.

'Naughty Tommy. He was never punished.'

'Was he not? Oh dear. We're off to walk by the river, are we going the right way?'

The old lady said nothing and stared at them.

'Well, if you don't mind, we'll be on our way,' said Mrs Moore

'Auntie Nellie!' came a cry from one of the cottages. They turned to see a lady walking towards them. She had long curly hair and wore a shawl and bonnet.

'I'm very sorry,' she said when she reached them. 'Auntie Nellie is a bit confused. Come on Nellie, let's go back inside.' She took the old lady's arm.

'She was telling us about naughty Tommy,' said Mrs Moore.

'Yes, she's talked about naughty Tommy for many years,' she said.

'Who is he?'

'Someone who once lived on the estate we think. Sadly, Auntie Nellie's husband died in the first Boer War, and she's never quite been the same since.'

'Frank?' said Aunt Nellie.

'Yes, Uncle Frank. We're all very sad he didn't come home again.' The old lady nodded, then looked Lottie and Mrs Moore up and down.

'I'm so sorry she troubled you,' said Auntie Nellie's niece. 'Thank you for not being rude to her.'

'Why would anyone be rude to her?'

'Oh, you know what some people are like.' The woman glanced at Hamilton Hall. 'Still, I mustn't speak ill of the dead. Come on Auntie Nellie, let's get you back inside. My name's Rosamund by the way.'

'I'm Roberta Moore and this is Lottie Sprigg.'

'It's lovely to meet you. I'll get Auntie back indoors now.'

They watched as she led the old lady back to the cottage.

'How sad she's lost her mind,' said Mrs Moore. 'I think that's probably my very worst fear, Lottie.'

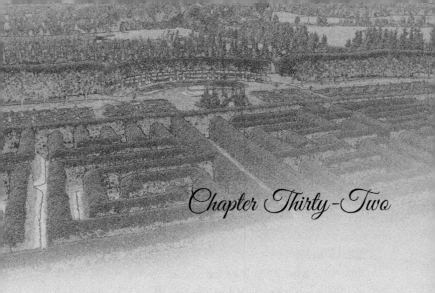

Chapter Thirty-Two

AFTER A PLEASANT RIVERSIDE WALK, Mrs Moore had a nap in her room. Lottie felt too restless to sit down with her book. She couldn't stop thinking about the gap in the maze wall. Could it have provided the perfect escape route for Lady Chichester's murderer?

She decided to look around for a ball of string to help her in the maze. She found Sally the maid in the corridor near her room and offered her condolences on the death of her employer.

'Thank you, Lottie. We're all very shocked.'

'Do you have any idea who could have done such a thing?' Lottie asked.

'No. I had one idea, but I think it's impossible.'

'What's your idea?'

'I shouldn't say, really. I don't want to get anyone into trouble.'

'But if they're a murderer, they should be in trouble!'

Sally smiled. 'That's a good point. I just don't want anyone to think I'm gossiping about them.'

'They needn't know.'

'I suppose not.' Sally lowered her voice. 'Just don't tell anyone I told you.'

'Alright.'

'Lady Forbes-Chichester,' whispered Sally. 'But only because she was here yesterday evening and was deliberately rude to Lady Chichester. I don't really believe Lady Forbes-Chichester would do such a thing. I enjoyed working for her. She was respectful and fair and I don't think she's a murderer. The trouble is...' She bit her lip as she thought. 'I don't know who else it could have been.'

'Hopefully the police will find out soon enough.'

'Yes, hopefully. I had to speak to the detective this morning, but I couldn't help him with anything. I was in the house when it happened and I didn't see anyone behaving suspiciously. I don't know how he's going to find out who did it.'

'He's got a lot of work to do,' said Lottie.

'He has. I don't suppose you've noticed any evidence of mice in your room, have you?'

'No.'

'One of the guests told the housekeeper they had mice in their room. I've visited all the bedrooms but can't see anything untoward.'

'I'll let you know if I see anything. Do you know if there's a ball of string somewhere I could borrow?'

'A ball of string?' Sally raised her eyebrows. Then she looked at Rosie. 'To use as a toy for your dog?'

Lottie nodded, even though it was a more suitable toy for a cat. 'Rosie likes string.'

'I'll go downstairs and see what I can find.'

A short while later, Lottie and Rosie walked around the perimeter of the maze again. It was early evening and the sunlight was the colour of deep gold.

When they reached the gap in the hedge, Lottie glanced around her. There was no one else in sight.

'Come on Rosie, let's go in.'

Lottie pushed herself through the hedge sideways. She screwed her eyes shut so she wouldn't be poked in the eye by a twig. The foliage scraped against her face and pulled at her clothes. She pulled herself free and stepped out onto a path in the maze.

'Come on, Rosie.' She parted the hedge as much as she could for the corgi to pass through.

Lottie then took the ball of string from her pocket and firmly tied the end to one of the little branches by the gap she had just pushed her way through. Now she felt reassured she'd be able to easily find her way out again.

'Which way shall we go?' Lottie looked left, then right. The hedges towered above her, and everything was silent. She couldn't even hear any birdsong. A cold tingle on the back of her neck made her want to leave.

'Come on Rosie, let's go left.' Lottie could hear the uncertainty in her voice. She held the ball of string loosely in one hand and allowed it to unravel as they walked. She'd heard flowers had been laid at the place where Lady Chichester had been attacked. All she had to do was determine how close the location was to the gap in the hedge.

Their walk resulted in a dead end, but Lottie rewound the ball of string to find her way back to the gap.

'It works, doesn't it Rosie? Let's try the other way now.' They passed the gap and continued on another route. Lottie walked quickly, feeling uneasy. There was an eeriness in the silence. They wound left and right and had to retrace their steps a few times.

They came across the flowers quite suddenly. Lottie felt a lump in her throat as she looked at the pretty bouquets propped up against the hedge. 'Poor Lady Chichester,' she said to Rosie. Then she gave a shudder. 'I don't think I want to stay here any longer. Let's see how long we take to get back to the gap.'

Lottie wound up the ball of string as they walked and felt relieved they would be out of the maze again soon.

Then she heard a noise.

Lottie stood still and held her breath. The sound had been unmistakable in the stillness of the maze. It had sounded like the scuff of a foot on the path.

Had she imagined it? She glanced around her. All she could see were yew hedges and the path she was on. The string stretched out ahead of her and Rosie stood silently by her side.

'Come on,' she whispered to her dog. 'Let's get out of here.'

She felt tempted to run, but she was wary of panicking too much. And perhaps it didn't matter there was someone else in the maze, everyone was entitled to stroll around it. Why had she assumed it was someone threatening?

With these thoughts, Lottie calmed herself. She continued to wind the string. 'I'm sure we're nearly there, Rosie.'

They followed the string around a corner and there it stopped.

Lottie gasped.

In the centre of the path ahead of her was a stone.

And tied around it was the end of her string.

Chapter Thirty-Three

'IT MUST HAVE BEEN someone having a joke,' said Mrs Moore. 'Not a very funny joke, but a joke all the same.'

Lottie was sitting in a chair in Mrs Moore's room and had just told her about her visit to the maze.

'How far was the stone from the gap in the hedge?' asked Mrs Moore.

'Luckily it wasn't very far.'

'The joker could have been quite mean and moved the end of the string to another part of the maze.'

'Thank goodness they didn't do that.'

Who had it been? Lottie felt sure now that she had heard the scuff of a foot in the maze. She hadn't been imagining it after all. The other person had known she was in there because they had seen the string. Why hadn't they called out a greeting? Or why hadn't they followed the string to find her? There was something sinister about the manner in which they had kept their identity secret. Although Mrs Moore thought it was someone having a joke, Lottie wasn't so sure. She found their behaviour more threatening than amusing.

'Perhaps it was Daisy Darby,' said Mrs Moore. 'There's

something odd about her, isn't there? She was keen to tell us that Maria Lawrence didn't like her or Lady Chichester. She's probably trying to spread some rumours so everyone will consider Maria Lawrence as the suspect.'

'So you think Miss Darby could be the murderer?' asked Lottie.

'I don't know. But it seemed to me she was attempting to manipulate our opinions. I'm always suspicious of anyone who tries to do that.'

'I've had a different thought,' said Lottie. 'I discovered this afternoon that the gap in the maze hedge is only a short walk from where Lady Chichester was attacked. I think the murderer could have used that route to quickly escape. And because the gap is on the opposite side of the maze to the terrace, they could have then run through the gardens down-hill to the river without being seen.'

'Someone must have seen them.'

'But maybe they didn't. Most of the guests seemed to be on the terrace at the time of the murder.'

'You're right, Lottie. And I squeezed through that gap before the murder happened so I didn't see anyone fleeing. But if the murderer used that route to escape, then that suggests they knew where they were going. The murderer must know the layout of the maze. In which case, it has to be Lord Chichester. What a thought! Could he really have done it?'

'Maybe. Or maybe not. The other person who knows the layout of the maze is his first wife.'

Chapter Thirty-Four

LADY ANNA FORBES-CHICHESTER glanced around at the garish yellow morning room and grimaced. It had once been furnished in a pleasing palette of blue and cream. But Ruby Higgins had changed it all and put some cheap-looking art on the walls. The fireplace had been boarded up and an ugly electric fire installed. The woman had no class!

Anna took in a breath and tried to calm herself. Every time she returned to her former home, she found something to be angry about.

Her former husband had been unbelievably stupid. And now Ruby Higgins was dead. He was going to be quite lost without her.

'When did you last see Lady Chichester, my lady?' asked Detective Inspector Wilson.

'When she was on the stage doing her silly singing and dancing.'

'You didn't see her after that?'

'No.'

'Did you go into the maze after the performance?'

'No. The footmen asked me to leave, so I had a brief conversation with my former husband and left.'

'What did you discuss with Lord Chichester?'

'It was only a quick conversation. He was disappointed that I'd ruined his wife's performance.'

'You weren't invited to the anniversary celebration, were you, my lady?'

'No, I wasn't.'

'But you turned up anyway.'

'Yes, I did. This was my home for over twenty years. My children grew up here. We had a happy existence until that woman came along.'

'And how did you hear about the celebration that was taking place this weekend?'

'From a friend. I realise it wasn't a good idea coming here. But the trouble is, I'm still angry. I was happy with my husband and she took it all away.'

'You wanted revenge?'

She chose her words carefully. 'Revenge is a nice idea, I suppose, but it doesn't change anything, does it? It doesn't make me feel better. I suppose I just wanted to cause some mischief. Mischief is more enjoyable. I knew it would upset Ruby Higgins if I jeered her. So that's what I did. But it's not the same thing as revenge.'

'So you left the premises before Lady Chichester was murdered?'

'Yes! I would never have harmed her. Jeering was enough for me. I'm obviously angry our marriage ended. And I'm angry I no longer live in this beautiful house. But murdering my husband's second wife would only make things worse, wouldn't it? I wouldn't wish to cut my life short and end up on the gallows. I couldn't commit murder, Detective. I don't believe any normal person could ever commit murder.'

'Some detectives believe anyone can be driven to it.'

'And do you believe that?'

'I'm not sure. Some murders are more cold-hearted than others. It's one thing to commit murder, but it's quite another to cunningly evade justice. I think both are acts of cold-heartedness. Perhaps any normal person might be driven to murder if they're really desperate. But can a normal person evade detection and lie to cover their tracks? No, I think that takes a special kind of skill. Evil even.'

'I agree, Detective. And for that reason, you must understand I couldn't possibly have murdered my former husband's new wife. I'm just not that sort of person.'

'Not even to punish your former husband for what he did to you?'

'No! You really need to understand I'm an ordinary lady who would never do such a thing. And besides, it would upset the family far too much. Despite everything my former husband has done, I still believe he can be a good father to our children. And now that he's grief stricken, he's going to find that difficult. I wouldn't have done anything to upset that.'

'Do you have any idea who would have done this?'

'None. But I can imagine Ruby Higgins made some enemies.'

'Lady Chichester, you mean.'

'I prefer to call her Ruby Higgins. And I know she will have upset many people. Your job is to find them, Detective. I wish I could help you a little more with it, but I can't.'

LOTTIE WOKE EARLY the following morning and took Rosie for a walk in the garden before breakfast.

What had happened to Lady Forbes-Chichester after she was removed from Hamilton Hall for interrupting Lady Chichester's performance? Lottie hadn't seen her since. She didn't even know if she lived locally.

Had Lady Forbes-Chichester left the estate after being escorted from the house? Or had she remained somewhere in the grounds, waiting for an opportunity to attack Lady Chichester?

If she had planned to attack Lady Chichester, then she must have known she'd gone into the maze. That suggested Lady Forbes-Chichester had lurked somewhere nearby, waiting to catch sight of her victim before following her. It wasn't impossible to imagine. She could have mingled with the crowd of guests. But surely someone would have spotted her? Especially as she'd just caused trouble in the ballroom.

Lottie believed it was possible Lady Forbes-Chichester had seen Lady Chichester enter the maze. If she had followed her in, then Lottie would have presumably encountered her after she had spoken to Lady Chichester. It was more likely Lady Forbes-Chichester had entered the maze through the gap in the hedge. And it was likely she'd left that way, too. The escape route would have been perfect for anyone keen to avoid the crowd of guests on the terrace.

So where was Lady Forbes-Chichester now? Were the police even considering her?

As Lottie and Rosie returned to the house, she noticed a smartly dressed young man at the back door. He was handing a large envelope to one of the footmen.

Conveniently, Rosie wished to sniff at some bushes close by, so Lottie gave her some time to do it while she listened to the conversation.

'Please ensure Mr Quentin Lawrence receives this immediately,' said the young man to the footman. 'And please inform him he's required to respond to Musgrave and Fingle at his very earliest convenience.'

'Musgrave and Fingle?'

'We're a solicitor's firm in London. I work as a clerk for the company and I came up by the first train this morning to deliver this by hand. Our previous attempts to contact Mr Lawrence have failed. I've been instructed to wait until you have handed the papers to him personally, then confirm to me you have done so.'

'Very well.'

Lottie had heard all she needed to. She made her way to the door and the two men moved to allow her and Rosie past. She thanked them, wished them both good morning and strolled towards the breakfast room.

'I CAN'T BELIEVE we're stuck here for the time being,' said Maria Lawrence at the breakfast table. 'Can't the detective understand we've got lives to be getting on with in London?'

Quentin sliced the top off his boiled egg. The yolk wasn't runny enough for his taste. 'I'm sure he's fully aware of it, darling. But he doesn't care, does he? When something like this happens, the police take it very seriously, and we've all got to do exactly as they say. It's an enormous inconvenience, but I suppose we should remember that a tragic event has occurred. They need to get to the bottom of it. Lord Chichester must be in an absolute state.' He summoned a footman and asked for another boiled egg.

'Oh, absolutely. Poor Lord Chichester,' said Maria. Her expression changed from irritation to concern as she realised she should express sympathy rather than complain. Quentin often had to remind her to think of others instead of just herself.

'I don't know why the police think we're any help, though,' she said. 'We saw nothing untoward.'

'It's what they do, isn't it? We have to stay here so we can all be questioned. It doesn't mean we're suspects, but we may have witnessed something which we didn't realise was suspicious at the time. Or we may have overheard something which we thought was meaningless but is actually of great importance. These detectives are very clever at working it out, you've got to hand it to them.'

The footman placed a new boiled egg in front of him. Then another footman appeared with a large envelope in his hand. 'Some urgent papers which it is requested must be delivered to you by hand, sir.'

'Thank you,' he said stiffly.

He didn't hold out a hand to receive them, so the footman placed the envelope on the table. 'The gentleman who delivered them has requested I inform him when you are in receipt of the papers, sir. Are you happy for me to do so?'

'I suppose so.' He caught Maria's eye. She was staring at him with a puzzled expression.

'Very good, sir.' The footman gave a bow and left.

'Why on earth is someone sending you urgent papers from London?' asked Maria.

'I don't know.'

'Why don't you open the envelope and find out?'

'Not at the breakfast table, darling. I'd like to enjoy my boiled egg first.'

'You didn't look very pleased when the footman came in with it. Are you expecting bad news?'

'No.' He sliced off the top of his egg to discover the yolk of this one wasn't runny enough, either. He thrust his spoon in anyway, keen to get on with his breakfast.

'I don't understand what can be so urgent that the papers are hand delivered to you at a place where you've been spending the weekend.'

He sighed. Maria wasn't giving up on the subject.

'Surely they can be delivered to your office for you to deal with on your return?' she added.

'Yes,' he said through gritted teeth. 'That would be the sensible thing to do, wouldn't it, darling? It's probably just lawyers.'

'Lawyers?'

'No need to look worried. It will be regarding a contract. You know what lawyers are like. They want everything done yesterday. And they never take a day off. Although, when you earn that much money, you don't really want a day off, do you?' He followed this with a chuckle to lighten the mood.

Maria finally returned to spreading marmalade on her toast. 'I think it's disgraceful. They should allow you to have a break. Don't they know what's happened to Lady Chichester?'

'Probably. But we're talking about lawyers, darling. It's a well-known fact that every one of them had his heart plucked from his chest cavity at birth and had it replaced with a lump of coal as black as a moonless night.'

'Ugh! Now you're putting me off my breakfast.'

'Sorry, darling.' He gave another chuckle and tried to ignore the discomfort brewing within.

Quentin knew full well what was in the envelope. Musgrave and Fingle had been pestering him for months. He hadn't responded to their letters and telephone calls, but now the papers had been hand delivered. And the footman had confirmed it with their messenger.

He'd done his best to ignore them, but his luck was running out.

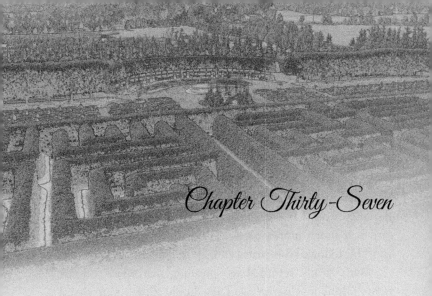

Chapter Thirty-Seven

'I was due to be in London for an important meeting today,' said Mrs Stanley-Piggot at breakfast. 'But I've had to postpone it now. I don't see why Detective Inspector Wilson insists on detaining us here.'

'Is it an important meeting?' asked Mrs Moore.

'I was supposed to be viewing another painting with my broker, Mr King.'

'A famous one?'

'Venus and Mars by Sandro Botticelli. It will have to remain in the National Gallery after I've bought it, but Mr King says that if we ask them nicely, they may allow a little plaque to be put on the wall next to it with my name on.'

'Is that so?'

As Mrs Stanley-Piggot continued to talk, Lottie watched the table where Mr and Mrs Lawrence sat. The large envelope from the solicitors Musgrave and Fingle lay untouched on the table. If the papers inside it were urgent, then why hadn't Mr Lawrence opened it yet?

He was eating a boiled egg with a tense expression on his

face. Mrs Lawrence didn't look particularly happy either. The urgent papers from the law firm seemed unwelcome. But why?

The polite chatter in the breakfast room died down when Lord Chichester appeared.

'Good morning everyone,' he said. 'I'm holding up and I slept a little better last night. I thought I'd mention it now to save each and every one of you asking. Thank you all for being so compliant with Detective Inspector Wilson. He's very much hoping to make a breakthrough today. And we need that, don't we?'

'We do indeed,' said Miss Darby with an appreciative clap. 'Would you like to join me over here, Lord Chichester?'

'Yes, I suppose I shall.' He passed Lottie's table on his way. 'Ah, Mrs Moore!' He stopped. 'I don't think I found the chance to ask you how your walk by the river was yesterday.'

'Oh, it was lovely, Lord Chichester, thank you. Miss Sprigg and I had a delightful time. It was such a beautiful afternoon. We met an interesting local character, actually. She lives in the workers' cottages.'

'Ah, yes.' His response seemed guarded.

'Nellie. An elderly lady who... well, sadly, she didn't speak a great deal of sense, but we spoke to her niece too.'

'Nellie Harrison,' said Lord Chichester. 'The poor old dear lost her marbles many moons ago. I believe she and her husband used to work on the estate, but she never recovered from his death in the first Boer War.'

'She talked about someone called Tommy.'

'Yes, that's quite typical of her. Apparently, she's been talking about him for years, but nobody knows who he is. She's as mad as a hatter. It must be very trying for the family. I once offered them some money for her to live in an institution, but they wouldn't accept it. They said she was far happier living on the estate with them. So there we have it.

There's no menace in her, she's just a little disconcerting if you haven't met her before. It's no kind of life having to look after someone like that, is it? I'm surprised the niece hasn't gone mad herself.'

Chapter Thirty-Eight

MR AND MRS LAWRENCE returned to their room after breakfast.

'Oh, I'm so bored here, Quentin!'

'Can't you use the time to learn some lines?'

'I know them off by heart.' She sighed. 'I could read the script again, though, and learn the lines of the other characters, too. Then I can prompt them when they forget their lines on the night. It's quite astonishing how often that happens, isn't it? Poor preparation.' She went over to her carpet bag by the dressing table. As she pulled the script out of it, there was a knock at the door and Quentin answered.

'Again?' she heard her husband say to someone. 'Very well.'

'The detective?' she asked him.

'Yes. He wants to speak to me again. I don't know why. He hasn't interviewed you yet, has he?'

'No. Although I'm sure my time will come. Good luck with it.'

'Thank you, darling.'

'Break a leg.'

He left and closed the door behind him.

The envelope.

Maria tossed her script onto the bed and looked around for it. Quentin had just left the room empty-handed. So where had he put the mysterious envelope?

She could steam the envelope open and find out what was inside it. She dashed into the bathroom which adjoined their room and ran the basin tap until it was as hot as she could possibly get it. Then she put the plug in the sink and filled the basin with hot water. She turned off the tap and watched the steam rise from the surface of the water. She didn't have long. The water would cool quickly and the steam would soon be lost again.

Maria skipped back into the bedroom and went to the chest of drawers where her husband stored his undergarments. Everything was carefully folded, so she did her best to keep it that way as she searched through.

There was no envelope.

She looked in the wardrobe, even though she hadn't recalled him opening it when they returned to the room. The envelope wasn't in there either. A suitcase was on top of the wardrobe. She pulled over a chair and stood on it, but the suitcase was empty.

She looked in the drawers of the writing desk. The envelope wasn't there.

She looked under the bed, under the bedcovers, under the pillows, and under the mattress.

Nothing.

She lifted the cushions on the easy chairs. Checked behind the curtains and looked under the rug. The envelope wasn't behind the mirror, nor was it behind a painting of a rural scene with sheep and shepherds.

Maria began pulling furniture away from the wall to find

out if her husband had tucked it behind something. There was no sign of it.

'What has he done with it?' she cried out in exasperation.

Perhaps it wasn't in the room at all. Had he left it on the breakfast table? Or maybe he'd hidden it somewhere en route from there.

She flung open her door only to find the occupant of the room opposite had done the same thing at the same time.

It was Miss Sprigg. The companion to the loud American, Mrs Moore.

The pair of them stared at each other for a moment. Both were equally surprised.

Miss Sprigg broke the silence first. 'Hello, Mrs Lawrence.'
'Hello.'

Maria glanced up and down the corridor. Where was the envelope?

She would have to trace her steps back to the breakfast room. She gave Miss Sprigg a nod and marched off.

Chapter Thirty-Nine

LOTTIE WATCHED Maria Lawrence storm off down the corridor.

'That was strange, Rosie,' she whispered. 'Mrs Lawrence looks very flustered. How embarrassing that we opened our doors at the same time as each other.'

Lottie had just received a shock of her own.

While she had been at breakfast, a note had been pushed under her door. She had opened her door just now to show the note to Mrs Moore. But the interruption from Mrs Lawrence had given her time to reconsider. It wasn't a very nice note and it would probably worry Mrs Moore to read it.

The note was written in a scrawling hand. As if someone had used the hand they didn't usually write with to disguise their handwriting:

Be careful in the maze. Do you know yew is poisonous?

Chapter Forty

THE ENVELOPE WAS NOWHERE to be found. After checking the breakfast room, Maria Lawrence went outside onto the terrace to clear her head.

It was quite obvious Quentin was lying to her, but she didn't understand why. What secrets could he possibly have? They usually told each other everything.

She couldn't fathom why a solicitor's firm would send a contract so urgently. And what made Quentin so sure the envelope contained a contract? He couldn't know without opening it. Why hadn't he opened it? And where on earth had he put it?

It could only mean Quentin was keeping something from her and he had no right to.

She followed a path, lost in her thoughts. As she approached the fountain, she realised Daisy Darby was there, and she was too close to pretend she hadn't seen her.

'Good morning, Miss Darby.'

'Good morning, Mrs Lawrence. Would you like a cigarette?'

Grudgingly, she accepted one. She had to make an effort to be polite, even though she felt sure Miss Darby didn't like her.

'Isn't it annoying being stuck here?' said Miss Darby.

'Yes it is, I was saying the same at breakfast. I suppose we have to be mindful of the recent tragic event and do all we can to help the police.'

'I'm worried that the longer I stay here, the more the detective is going to suspect me.'

'Because you were there when it happened?'

'Yes. He might decide I made the story up about the hand coming through the hedge, mightn't he? And I haven't helped myself because I accidentally spoke out of turn before Ruby died.'

'What did you say?'

'I complained to a few people about your husband's plans to turn the Pom-Pom Duo into a trio. And I also mentioned Ruby got more attention than me.'

'You're right. She did.'

Miss Darby met her gaze. 'Thank you, Mrs Lawrence. I'm pleased you believe it too. For so long I wondered whether I was imagining things. But it's fair to say your husband completely doted on her, didn't he?'

'Yes.'

'So I really was second best, and I was right to feel bad about it! Good.' She looked away again and inhaled on her cigarette.

'Presumably you're worried that people think you were jealous of Ruby.'

'Yes. And I wasn't. I was just annoyed because she got pref-erential treatment.'

The fact Miss Darby had been moaning about Ruby before her death didn't look good. She was certainly at risk of landing herself in trouble. Maria couldn't resist a little smile to herself.

'Surely it must have annoyed you too?' said Miss Darby.

'What did?'

'Your husband making such a fuss of Ruby like that. Didn't it worry you?'

Maria felt a bitter taste in her mouth. 'No,' she lied.

'Well, that's very accommodating of you. I think some wives would be very fed up if their husband was completely enchanted by a young woman.'

'I suppose you speak from experience,' said Maria. Daisy Darby was always flinging herself at rich men in the hope one of them would leave his wife and marry her.

'Lord Moorcroft and I are just friends!' said Miss Darby.

'Very well. And the relationship between Ruby and my husband was purely professional,' said Maria coldly. 'Nothing more.' She couldn't possibly allow anyone to think she had resented Ruby Higgins.

'Your husband must be worried too,' said Miss Darby.

'About what?'

'About the argument he and Ruby had about her performance.'

'That was normal.'

'It was normal for them to argue. But she was very upset about it on this occasion because he had been so picky about her performance in her own home.'

'You know what my husband is like, Miss Darby. He's a perfectionist. And you know yourself that their disagreements were common. You need to be careful what you tell the detective.'

'Why?'

'Because detectives jump to the wrong conclusions. And it's irrelevant. It has nothing to do with Ruby's death.'

'What makes you so sure?'

'Because my husband had absolutely nothing to do with it.

You've admitted you were complaining about Ruby before her death. So I'm afraid you had a motive.'

'I didn't murder her! Your husband had a stronger motive than me.'

'Nonsense.'

'Ruby knew something about him.'

'What?'

'I don't know. She said she'd tell me one day, but she didn't want to put an end to the Pom-Pom Duo.'

'You never found out?'

'No. He's your husband, Mrs Lawrence. Why don't you ask him yourself?'

WHO HAD WRITTEN the note which had been pushed under Lottie's door? It mentioned the maze. Did that mean it had been written by someone who knew Lottie had gone back to the maze? Was it the same person who'd tied her piece of string to the stone?

Mrs Moore had warned her to be careful. But it seemed someone knew she was trying to investigate the murder.

Lottie had to be cautious. But she also resolved to get one step ahead of the person who'd written the note.

The Lawrences were obvious suspects. Their room was opposite hers, so they would have found it easy to push a note beneath her door. And the large envelope which had been delivered that morning had clearly been unwelcome. Mr Lawrence hadn't opened it. Was that because he had something to hide? His wife was behaving oddly. Why had she given Lottie a strange look, then run off down the corridor?

Lottie was desperate to know what was in the envelope. And fortunately, she had a plan to find out.

'I need a telephone,' she said to Rosie.

The pair went downstairs and Lottie glanced in a few rooms, hoping there was a telephone she could use in privacy.

There was a telephone in the entrance hall at the foot of the stairs, but it wasn't private at all. Anyone could walk past and hear what she was saying. There was no telephone in the library. She knew there was one in the morning room, but the detective and police sergeant were in there. The sitting room had guests in it, but the peach and gold drawing room was empty.

Lottie crept in with Rosie by her side. A telephone was sitting on a small occasional table next to a sofa. It was difficult to imagine anyone using the drawing room at this time of day, but Lottie was aware the maids could come in at any time to attend to some housekeeping.

She walked up to the table and realised that if she sat on the floor, tucked up against the wall, she would be hidden from the view of anyone who walked into the drawing room. Cautiously, she lifted the telephone down from the table and sat on the floor with it by her side.

Rosie sat facing her. If it was possible for the corgi to look puzzled, then that was what she was doing at this moment.

'Here we go Rosie.' Lottie took in a deep breath and dialled the operator. Then she asked to be put through to Musgrave and Fingle's offices in London. Her heart thudded heavily as she listened to the distant ringing tone.

Then there was an answer. 'Musgrave and Fingle Solicitors, how may I help?' It was a perfunctory female voice.

Lottie adopted the politest accent she could muster. 'Oh, good morning. My name is Miss Bovis, and I'm telephoning on behalf of my employer, Mr Lawrence. He's currently staying at Hamilton Hall in Buckinghamshire and received some documents from you this morning. They were hand-delivered.'

'Mr Quentin Lawrence?'

'Yes, that's right. And I'm afraid there's been a terrible mishap.'

'Oh dear. What's happened?'

'He opened the documents at breakfast time and, unfortunately, there was an incident with the teapot. Tea was spilled absolutely everywhere, I'm afraid. And sadly, the covering letter is quite illegible now.'

'I see. Did Mr Lawrence have an opportunity to read the letter?'

'No. He had only just begun reading it. So he doesn't yet know what the letter says. He's asked me to telephone you to clarify the contents of the letter so I can tell him.'

'Right.' The response sounded slightly irritated. 'I shall make some inquiries. Are you alright to wait?'

Lottie glanced nervously about. The drawing room was still empty, but someone could come in at any moment. She prayed they wouldn't.

'Yes. I'm happy to wait. Thank you.'

She heard rustling, then distant voices. Then more rustling. Lottie had been half-expecting the lady at the other end of the telephone to disbelieve her. But the ruse appeared to be working.

Her palms felt damp as she waited. Perhaps she would be found out after all?

A minute passed and Lottie felt tempted to hang up the receiver. Surely someone was going to discover her here soon?

'Hello Miss Bovis, are you there?'

'Yes, I am here,' said Lottie.

'I have a copy of the letter which was sent to Mr Lawrence in front of me. It is regarding our client, Mr Foster.'

'Oh yes. Please can you remind me who he is again?'

'He's the gentleman who wrote the songs.'

'The songs?'

'Yes. The book of songs which were left on the train.'

Lottie's eyes widened at this news. But she remained calm, as if she'd heard it all before. 'Oh yes. I remember now.'

'The letter is quite succinct. I'm not sure why Mr Lawrence struggled to read it.'

'Well, there was an awful lot of tea.'

'I see. The letter merely requests that he visit our offices at his earliest convenience. Our client is reluctant to take this matter to court, but he is more than prepared to if a settlement can't be reached. So you must stress to your employer, Mr Lawrence, that it really is in his interests to reach a settlement with us.'

'You mean money?'

'Yes. A financial settlement which will include legal fees. And a public apology.'

'Public?' Lottie understood now why Mr Lawrence was a reluctant recipient of the letter.

'Yes. A public apology. In fact, if you could put Mr Lawrence on the line now, I can ask Mr Musgrave to explain it to him in more detail.'

'That won't be possible, I'm afraid,' said Lottie. 'He's currently speaking to a detective. I take it you've heard about the tragic incident at Hamilton Hall?'

'Yes, we have read about it in the newspapers. Please pass on our condolences to the family.'

'I will do.'

'I imagine it may be a few days before Mr Lawrence is back in London?'

'Yes.'

'In which case, it really is important that he telephones us. Can you ask him to do so today? The matter really cannot continue to drag on.'

'Of course.' Lottie felt keen to get off the telephone now.

'Wonderful. I shall inform Mr Musgrave that he can expect Mr Lawrence's telephone call today.'

Someone stepped into the room.

'Wonderful,' said Lottie. 'Thank you for cancelling the tickets.'

'Tickets?'

Lottie hung up the receiver and exhaled a long breath.

'Miss Sprigg?' said Sally the maid. 'What are you doing down there?'

'I had to make a telephone call to cancel Mrs Moore's theatre tickets for tonight.'

'Oh, that's a shame. What was she going to see?'

Lottie had to think quickly again. 'Macbeth at the Princess Theatre in London.'

'Oh yes. The production which Mrs Lawrence didn't get the part of Lady Macbeth for. Everyone below stairs has been talking about that.'

'Have they? I thought Mrs Lawrence said she didn't go for it.'

'She would say that, wouldn't she? But the rumour is Lady Chichester intervened. It's no secret the two didn't get on.'

'I've heard that. Why do people think Lady Chichester intervened?'

'Her maid overhead her discussing it with Lord Chichester. Anyway, I shouldn't gossip too much. Why are you sitting on the floor, Miss Sprigg?'

'I was hiding. I wasn't sure if I was allowed to use this telephone.'

'Of course you are! You're one of the guests. Perhaps you sometimes forget you're not a maid anymore?'

'Yes.' Lottie smiled. 'I do forget that sometimes.'

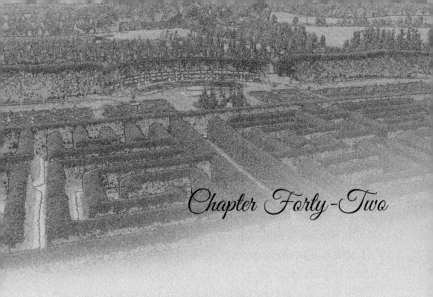

Chapter Forty-Two

'GOODNESS LOTTIE, that was brazen of you!' said Mrs Moore as they walked together in the garden. Lottie had just told her about her telephone call with the solicitor's firm. 'I don't think I'd have the confidence to telephone somewhere pretending to be someone else.'

'The lady at the firm told me they were acting on behalf of Mr Foster who left a book of songs on the train. That suggests Mr Lawrence took the book, doesn't it?'

'Yes, it does.'

'I wonder if he then used the songs in the book as his own?'

'That explains the request for a financial settlement and a public apology,' said Mrs Moore. 'Both quite punitive for Mr Lawrence, no doubt.'

'This could be what Lady Chichester was referring to during their argument,' said Lottie. 'When he explained it to us all, he tried to pass it off as a joke about his mother writing his songs. But she could have known he stole that book of songs and used them as his own. She said to him, "if you don't stop bullying me, I shall tell people where you got your songs from."'

'This must be what she was talking about! And just imagine what would happen to him if everyone found out. Perhaps he could reach a financial settlement. But a public apology would ruin him, wouldn't it? That would be the end of his career. No one would be happy his songs had been stolen from a book he found on a train. In fact, you wonder if he has written any of his songs at all.'

'It would be interesting to hear Mr Foster's side of the story,' said Lottie. 'I wonder who he is?'

'No doubt he's a jobbing writer who has nowhere near the amount of money and fame as Mr Lawrence. But he's done the sensible thing and consulted a firm of lawyers. And Mr Lawrence is quite obviously unhappy about it. I wonder if he's told his wife?'

'She didn't look very happy earlier. So perhaps he did, or perhaps she's still wondering what's in the envelope.'

Mrs Moore chuckled. 'And to think you told the law firm that he'd spilled his tea all over the letter. That was quite ingenious of you, Lottie.'

'But this could mean Mr Lawrence is the murderer, couldn't it? Lady Chichester threatened to reveal his secret. Perhaps he decided to silence her.'

'It's a strong motive for murder. And sometimes when you mention a suspect's name, I respond by saying I couldn't imagine them doing such a thing. Unfortunately, on this occasion, I can imagine Mr Lawrence doing something unpleasant like that. He's the sort of man who's only interested in himself. I suppose the theatre world is full of men like that. And ladies too. But there's something about him I don't like. Are you going to share this information with the police?'

'I think I have to. But I shall do it anonymously.'

'How?'

'I'll write a note for the detective. And if he thinks there's something in it, then he can telephone the law firm and speak to Mr Foster too, if necessary. But I don't want to tell the detective in person. I'm worried Mr Lawrence will find out it was me.'

'That's fair enough, Lottie.'

She pulled the note she'd received from her pocket. 'And if Mr Lawrence is the murderer, then I think he wrote this note.' She showed it to her employer.

Mrs Moore's jaw dropped. '"Be careful in the maze. Do you know yew is poisonous?" Good grief, Lottie! Someone sent you this note?'

Lottie nodded.

'I don't like this at all,' said Mrs Moore. 'I think you need to show this to the detective.'

'Not yet,' said Lottie. 'I'll send him my note first. Then we can see what happens.'

WHERE WAS THE ENVELOPE? Maria Lawrence still hadn't found it. And to make matters worse, she was now being interviewed by Detective Inspector Wilson. His companion, an officious-looking police sergeant, was writing down her every word.

'How well did you know Lady Chichester?' asked the detective.

'It seems so funny when people call her that. I'm still in the habit of referring to her as Ruby Higgins. She was Ruby Higgins when she first met my husband and me.'

'And when was that?'

'Two years ago. For some reason, and I really don't know why, we went to the Hackney Empire. It was a fleapit, as you can imagine. But I will admit there were some talented performers that night. Music hall entertainment is not my thing, but some of it was quite good. Ruby Higgins stole the show as one half of the Pom-Pom Duo. And from that moment, my husband was entranced. It was always apparent that Ruby was the more talented of the two. Don't tell Miss Darby I said that, will you?'

'And then?'

'My husband took them on. He did everything for them. He managed them, wrote their songs, chose their outfits... you name it. And they were enormously successful. It was all thanks to Quentin and I don't believe he ever received a proper thank you for it.'

'He made good money?'

'Yes. Quite good.'

'Your husband appears to have been very fond of Lady Chichester.'

'Yes, he was. But purely on a professional level. There is absolutely no suggestion that anything untoward ever happened between them. I trust my husband implicitly. Ruby Higgins, as we know, has perhaps been a little less trustworthy when you consider she had an affair with Lord Chichester, who was married to someone else at the time. But nevertheless, she took her job seriously, and was actually very professional about it.'

'And how did you get on with Lady Chichester?'

'Very well. We were quite different from each other. Different backgrounds. She ended up a lady, but she was born in Bermondsey. Despite that, we found enough in common that we could get along all right.'

She gave the detective a smile, but even though she was an actress, it wasn't easy to make it seem genuine. Talking about Ruby Higgins made her jaw tighten.

'And where were you at the time of the murder, Mrs Lawrence?'

'I didn't murder her!'

His eyes narrowed. 'I merely asked where you were at the time of the murder.'

'I was in the maze. Like everyone else.'

'Not everyone was in the maze at the time.'

'Well, a lot of people were.'

'Did you see Lady Chichester in the maze?'

'No.'

His eyes narrowed further. The more he questioned her, the angrier she felt. She tried to calm herself but couldn't.

'I didn't want to come here for this silly anniversary weekend, you know,' she said. 'It was the last thing I wanted to do!'

'But your husband did want to come here?'

'Yes. Unfortunately, he did.'

'What's that?' The detective looked past her to the door.

Maria turned to see a piece of paper pushed beneath it.

'Travers,' said the detective. 'Go and fetch that, please.'

Detective Inspector Wilson summoned everyone to the drawing room that afternoon.

'I wonder if this has something to do with your note, Lottie,' whispered Mrs Moore as they made their way there with Rosie.

Tea and sandwiches had been laid out on a table in the drawing room and Daisy Darby was busying herself with the teapot.

'Everyone for tea?' she called out.

People murmured their thanks.

'Well, considering this is a house of mourning, the staff are managing to put on a good spread,' said Quentin Lawrence.

Lord Chichester gave a sad nod. 'Yes, the housekeeper has always ensured this place is impeccably run. I don't know how she does it. She and all the staff are saddened by what's happened to my wife, and yet they go about their work just as efficiently as ever. I really am very lucky to have them.'

'And you have your family for comfort too, Lord Chichester,' said Mrs Lawrence.

'I don't have a great deal of family, I'm afraid. I inherited this place from a great uncle of mine who I barely knew. I was an only child. I have a few uncles remaining, but I haven't seen them for many years.'

'Well, at least you have this wonderful estate,' said Mrs Lawrence. 'I suppose that's a comfort.'

'Oh yes, it must be,' said Mrs Stanley-Piggot. 'In fact, I'd like to buy an estate similar to this. I love the space you get with these country estates. Lots of land and few neighbours.'

'You still have neighbours, Margaret, you just can't see them from your house,' said Lord Chichester. 'But believe me, they can cause trouble if they want to. Whether it's bickering over a boundary or access to a certain track. And you have to put up with people living on your estate too. I have some tenants whose families once worked for the Chichester family but no longer do so. They've got a clause in their tenancy agreement which means they can inhabit their residences until they die. So that's a bit of a shame. They can be a nuisance sometimes.'

'In what way, Lord Chichester?' asked Mrs Moore.

'I suspect it comes down to simple jealousy. They see someone in a manor house and they want the same for themselves. But that's quite ridiculous, isn't it? If everyone lived on an estate like this, there simply wouldn't be space for all of us. I'm afraid it's a fact of life. We can't change what we've been born into.'

'Indeed we can't,' said Miss Darby. Lottie detected a note of regret in her tone.

'Life is unequal,' said Lord Chichester. 'But what would we do without the ruling classes? The country would be in utter mayhem. And we need the working classes just as much, too. We need people to till the land and make goods in our factories. Without them, the country would stop too.'

'And we also need the middle classes,' said Mrs Moore.

'Like lawyers and other professionals.' She gave Mr Lawrence a sidelong glance, and he shifted uncomfortably in his seat.

'Absolutely, Mrs Moore,' said Lord Chichester. 'Between us all, we keep the country ticking over, don't we? So we simply cannot begrudge each other's position in life. Some people struggle to accept where they are on the social ladder, but it's a simple fact of life, isn't it? You find just the same in the animal and plant kingdom.'

'Plants have a social ladder?' asked Mrs Moore.

'No. But some plants are dominant and take over an entire border.'

'Like people?'

'Some people I suppose.'

'If a dominant plant takes over my border, then I rip it up,' said Mrs Lawrence.

'Golly,' said Mrs Moore. 'Don't you leave just a little bit of it?'

'No.'

'If anyone's comparing a dominant plant to the ruling classes, then I shall state that I absolutely believe in being held accountable for my actions,' said Lord Chichester. 'Every member of the ruling class should be. We have an important role and should be answerable to the people lower down.'

'Interesting,' said Mrs Stanley-Piggot in a disinterested voice. 'But let's return to my question. In your opinion, Lord Chichester, where might be a good place to buy a country estate?'

'You could do quite well here in Buckinghamshire, Mrs Stanley-Piggot. There are several pleasant properties here. And London is just a short trip away.'

'There's a rather nice castle in Berkshire,' said Miss Darby, pouring out the tea.

'Is there?'

'Yes. It's very old. I think its earliest buildings were built by William the Conqueror.'

'Goodness me, that sounds nice.'

'It occupies a prominent position in the town of Windsor.'

Mr Lawrence gave a laugh. 'You mean Windsor Castle, Miss Darby? A residence of the royal family?'

'Yes, it's their residence at the moment. But I'm sure Mr Jones, the broker, would do you a good deal, Mrs Stanley-Piggot.'

The older lady's lips pursed. 'Very amusing, I'm sure.'

Miss Darby handed out the tea and everyone settled themselves in chairs around a large coffee table.

'Let's hope that detective arrives shortly,' said Lord Chichester. 'He's late.'

Detective Inspector Wilson turned up a few minutes later with Sergeant Travers in tow.

'Well done, everyone,' he said. 'I realise you're all fed up with speaking to me, but that's the way it goes, I'm afraid.' He pulled a piece of paper from his pocket and held it above his head. 'I would like to find out the author of this anonymous note.'

THERE WAS silence in the drawing room. Lottie's face heated up, and she prayed nobody would notice.

'No one?' said Detective Inspector Wilson, waving the note about.

Lord Chichester glanced around the room. 'No one,' he said. 'What does the note say?'

'It reveals some rather interesting information. It has led me to make a few inquiries which, in fact, support the information in this note. And I'd be very interested to know who passed this to me.'

Lottie sat still, holding her breath. She sensed Mrs Moore next to her was doing the same.

'I don't think anybody here wrote it, Detective,' said Lord Chichester. 'Tell us what it's all about.'

'Very well. It's regarding Mr Lawrence.'

'Me?' said Mr Lawrence. 'Who's been writing anonymous notes about me?'

'If only I could answer your question, Mr Lawrence,' said the detective. 'I take it you heard me describe the note as anonymous?'

'Yes. It's an outrage!'

'I can only imagine this person wishes to remain anonymous for fear of retribution,' said the detective.

Lottie leaned forward and nonchalantly picked up her cup of tea from the coffee table. She prayed the mysterious Miss Bovis, who had phoned the solicitor's firm, wouldn't be mentioned. Although she was pleased the detective had followed up on her note, she felt uncomfortable. She felt sure something in her face or gestures would give her away.

'When have I ever carried out any retribution against anyone?' asked Mr Lawrence.

'I don't know you well enough to say,' replied the detective. 'Anyway, this note states that you've had some communication from some lawyers representing a Mr Foster. Would you care to explain who Mr Foster is?'

'Never heard of him.'

'Alright then. I shall elaborate further. This note contains the name of a London solicitor's firm which has been attempting to contact you regarding its client, Mr Foster.'

'I don't know anything about it.' Mr Lawrence sat with his arms folded and his nose in the air.

'When I first read this note, I wondered if it was an attempt to thwart my investigation. But I decided a telephone call to the solicitor's firm would soon clarify that. I spoke to a chap called Mr Musgrave.'

'I've no idea who he is.'

'He told me his client, Mr Foster, is a struggling songwriter. He's written a good deal of songs, but he's not had a lot of personal success yet. I'm not very familiar with the world of show business, but my impression is that it helps to know the right people. If you know the right people, then your work gets more publicity. Anyway, about a year ago, Mr Foster was returning home on the tube train from Leicester Square to Kennington when he accidentally left his book of songs on the train. He was understandably dismayed. Apparently, he's tried to rewrite many of the songs as he remembers them. But he maintains nothing will ever replace what he lost that day.'

'If those songs were so precious to him, why did he leave them on the tube train?' said Lord Chichester.

'An exceptionally well-made point!' said Mr Lawrence. 'Thank you, Lord Chichester.'

Mrs Moore picked up her cup of tea from the coffee table but stopped before she took a sip from it. 'Sorry,' she whispered to Mrs Stanley-Piggot. 'I accidentally picked up yours.' She handed it to her.

'The solicitor, Mr Musgrave, informed me Mr Foster had taken the book of songs to a meeting with an agent in the West End,' said the detective. 'It's unfortunate he left the book on the train. Perhaps he could have made copies of his songs, but that's the beauty of hindsight. Anyway, he left the book of songs on the train and someone found the book. But instead of handing the book into the lost property office at a station, that person took the book home with him and claimed the songs as his own.'

'No!' said Mrs Lawrence, clasping her hand to her chest. 'Is this true, Quentin? You stole those songs?'

'No. I didn't steal them. I didn't forcibly remove them from his hand. I found them.'

'You should have handed the book into the lost property office.'

'I didn't think it would be valuable to anyone. It looked like it was just filled with scribble.'

'But it wasn't scribble was it, Mr Lawrence?' said the detective. 'Mr Musgrave informed me a number of the stolen songs were performed by the Pom-Pom Duo. And am I also right in thinking you have earned good money from the performances of those songs?'

Mr Lawrence gave a snort. 'I don't know why everyone is so convinced the Pom-Pom Duo has made me rich.'

'You made far more money than I ever did!' said Daisy Darby. 'And you didn't even write the songs!' Her eyes were red. Lottie imagined she felt betrayed.

'Apparently Mr Foster realised his songs had been stolen when he heard one of them being performed by the Pom-Pom Duo in a West End theatre,' said the detective. 'What do you have to say to that, Mr Lawrence?'

'There's no need for you to question me in front of everyone like I'm on trial, Detective!'

'But is it true, Quentin?' asked his wife. 'You stole those songs and passed them off as your own?'

'It's not that simple, Maria.'

'No, I expect it's not. Nothing is ever simple with you, is it? No wonder you didn't want to open that envelope which arrived for you this morning. Presumably it contains all the legal papers regarding your theft!'

'I didn't steal any songs, Maria!' protested Mr Lawrence. 'I merely found a notebook which had scribbles in it.'

'Which you then turned into successful performances,' said Detective Inspector Wilson.

'But what are the chances of a songwriter finding songs written by another songwriter left on a tube train? Very unlikely. I didn't realise Mr Foster was a hard-working song-writer who had struggled to find success with his songs. If I had known that, then I wouldn't have taken the songbook. I just assumed it had been left behind on purpose. I thought nobody wanted it anymore.'

'I suppose it all boils down to what the definition of theft is,' said Lord Chichester.

'Exactly! I don't call it theft. However, Mr Foster and his solicitors are calling it theft. I call it finders keepers.'

'But there's also the fact that you passed off the work as your own,' said the detective.

'Is that a crime?'

'It's deceitful. And it's clearly something you didn't want anybody else to find out about.'

'What makes you say that?'

'Because even your own wife didn't know you found this book of songs on the tube train and used them as your own.'

'I didn't tell Maria because I didn't think she would be interested.'

'Of course I'd be interested, Quentin! And if you'd told me about it, I would have told you to hand the book into the lost property office.'

'I thought someone didn't need the book anymore and then I was inspired by the scribblings I found within it to create my music. It really is that simple. Anyway, who's going to own up to writing the anonymous note?' Mr Lawrence glanced around him.

There was no reply.

'Someone who's clearly not in the room with us now,' said the detective. 'For the time being, it seems they shall remain incognito. But they have provided some very useful information.'

'If it's true, then it's very unsavoury indeed,' said Lord Chichester. 'I thought better of you, Lawrence. But even if it is true, what does it have to do with my wife's murder?'

The detective eyed Mr Lawrence. 'That all depends, my lord.'

'On what?'

'On whether Lady Chichester knew those songs had been stolen.'

'They weren't stolen!'

'Lady Chichester told you she was going to tell people where your songs came from.'

'Yes, that was the joke about my mother.'

'I don't think it was though, was it Mr Lawrence? I think Lady Chichester knew about Mr Foster's stolen book. Did you confess it to her?'

'No! There was nothing to confess! I may have mentioned that some of my songs had been inspired by a book I'd found discarded on the tube.'

'So you did steal the songs and Lady Chichester knew,' said the detective. 'She threatened to tell people you stole the songs and that could have caused a lot of trouble for you, couldn't it? It could have ended your career. Did you silence her, Mr Lawrence?'

'No.' He picked up his cup of tea from the coffee table and gulped it down.

'Are you sure about that?'

'Yes.' His reply sounded slightly strangulated.

'Are you alright, Mr Lawrence?'

'No. What was in that tea? It tasted gritty...'

As he trailed off, his face went a horrible red colour.

'Mr Lawrence?' said Mrs Stanley-Piggot. 'What's wrong?'

'Oh my goodness, Quentin!' Mrs Lawrence rose from her seat. 'Are you alright? It looks like you're struggling to breathe.'

Quentin Lawrence gave a gasp, clutched at his throat, then tumbled forward onto the coffee table.

Chapter Forty-Six

A DOCTOR WAS SUMMONED, and everyone was ushered outside onto the terrace.

'Good golly,' said Mrs Moore. 'This is terrible! What do you suppose is the matter with Quentin Lawrence? It must be the shock of getting found out.'

'Do you think his heart gave out?' said Mrs Stanley-Piggot.

'He said there was something gritty in his tea,' said Lottie.

'Poison?' said Miss Darby.

'No!' said Mrs Moore. 'Surely not! Someone in the drawing room put poison in his tea?'

Lottie thought of the note she'd received. It had mentioned yew being poisonous. Had the author of that note poisoned Mr Lawrence? Could Lottie be next?

An icy shiver ran down her spine.

'All the cups of tea were on the coffee table,' said Mrs Moore. 'Surely we would have noticed if someone had put poison in one of the cups.'

'Or would we?' said Mrs Stanley-Piggot. 'I was quite distracted by the conversation, so I wasn't always looking.'

'And with people picking up their cups and putting them

down again and using the ashtray and all the rest of it,' said Miss Darby, 'I think someone could have managed it if they were clever enough.'

'I struggle to believe it,' said Mrs Moore. 'Oh, here comes Lord Chichester now.'

His face was solemn.

'The doctor has seen to him,' he said. 'And I'm afraid it's bad news.'

'Mr Lawrence is dead?' said Miss Darby.

'I'm afraid so. And the detective wants us all in the sitting room now.'

Detective Inspector Wilson paced the room as they took their seats. His expression was thunderous and Lottie suspected he was angry someone had been brazen enough to commit murder beneath his nose.

Mrs Lawrence joined them and sat herself down as she dabbed at her eyes with a handkerchief.

'Not many suspects,' said the detective, eyeing them all. 'I'll easily find out which one of you did this. Mark my words.'

Lottie felt like she was in trouble, even though she'd done nothing wrong.

There was a knock at the door, and Sergeant Travers entered.

'I'm in the middle of addressing the suspects, Travers.'

'I thought you might like to see this, sir.' He handed him a small box. Detective Inspector Wilson turned it over in his hand and examined it.

'Rat poison,' he said eventually. 'Where did you find this, Travers?'

'In a large blue and white vase.'

'That sounds like the Ming vase,' said Lord Chichester.

'So this could be the poison used to murder Mr

Lawrence,' said the detective. 'It's clear to me this packet has been opened. Would anyone like to own up to it?'

He held up the box and everyone in the room remained silent.

'No volunteers,' said the detective with a sigh. 'Let me give you a warning. The longer you leave this, the worse it will get for you. I'm giving you an opportunity now to come clean. But if you choose not to take it, then on your own head be it.'

'Was the pot of tea poisoned?' asked Mrs Stanley-Piggot.

'I don't think so,' said the detective. 'Otherwise you'd all be dead, wouldn't you? Someone put poison into Mr Lawrence's cup! Some of the residue is still in it.'

'Someone must have sneaked in and done it,' said Lord Chichester. 'I don't believe a single person in this room could have carried out that murder. Or the previous murder! This has to be the work of an interloper who's extremely good at hiding.'

'They'd have to be exceptionally good,' said the detective. 'Because I have no idea how they got into the drawing room this afternoon with none of us noticing. I don't think this is the work of an interloper, Lord Chichester. I think it's one of you sitting in front of me now!'

Chapter Forty-Seven

'WHAT A DAY!' said Mrs Moore as she and Lottie sat on her balcony. It was early evening and the shadows in the maze were growing deeper as the sun lowered in the sky. 'We found out Quentin Lawrence was a fraud and then he died! Quite shocking.'

Rosie sat by Lottie's feet. She patted the corgi on the head, deep in thought. 'Miss Darby poured the tea, didn't she?'

'You're right, she did! And she was in the maze with Lady Chichester.'

'But how did Miss Darby put poison in Mr Lawrence's tea?' said Lottie.

'I think it might be easier than we realise. We were all quite squashed around that coffee table, weren't we? At one point, I accidentally picked up Mrs Stanley-Piggot's tea, thinking it was mine.'

'So the poisoner could have done the same but used the opportunity to put poison in the tea!' said Lottie. She closed her eyes for a moment and thought back to the afternoon. 'I wish I could remember if I saw someone do something like that.'

'I'm trying to remember too,' said Mrs Moore. 'Hopefully, a memory will come back to us. That's all we need. Just a small recollection.'

'If it is Miss Darby,' said Lottie. 'Then why did she murder Quentin Lawrence?'

'She told us how discontented she was, didn't she? Perhaps she was so unhappy in her work that she decided to get rid of the two people she worked with.'

'But what would she gain from that?'

'Freedom, perhaps,' said Mrs Moore. 'She was tied into a contract, wasn't she? That's presumably null and void now. The Pom-Pom Duo is no more and her manager is dead too. But what an occasion to try out such a trick. The wedding anniversary of Lord Chichester and his wife. To murder a young woman on the day of her wedding anniversary and then murder the man who'd helped her become successful. Why choose to do it here? Surely she could have carried it out when they were in London.'

'Because there are other guests here. There are other people to blame.'

'I see what you're saying, Lottie. A good tactic. Perhaps she hoped other people would be suspected above her. But could she really have been that desperate? Who else is there to consider?'

'Maria Lawrence. She was very upset her husband had lied to her.'

'But she only found that out shortly before he was poisoned.'

'I think she suspected he'd been lying to her sooner. Those papers from the law firm bothered her, and I saw her this morning acting strangely.'

'In what way?'

'We opened our bedroom doors at the same time as each other and her eyes were wide and staring. Then she muttered something to herself and dashed off down the corridor.'

'You think she could have been plotting to murder her husband then?'

'Possibly. She was behaving oddly.'

'But why would she murder Lady Chichester?'

'They didn't get on.' Lottie now recalled something Sally the maid had told her earlier. 'And apparently, Lady Chichester intervened to stop Maria Lawrence getting the role of Lady Macbeth at the production that's currently on at the Princess Theatre.'

'No! Where did you hear that?'

'From Sally the maid. She heard it from Lady Chichester's maid who'd overheard a conversation between Lady Chichester and her husband.'

'Servant gossip can be very useful indeed!' said Mrs Moore. 'Although we can't always be sure it's true. If it is true, then Maria Lawrence could be the murderer. She murdered Lady Chichester out of revenge and her husband because he lied to her. Could that really be the case, though? We have to think about other people too. Margaret Stanley-Piggot. Why would she murder Lady Chichester?'

'She said it was a shame Lord Chichester's first marriage ended.'

'That's right. She did. Is that enough reason to murder the Second Lady Chichester?'

'I don't think so. Unless the first Lady Chichester is a very good friend of hers and she sought revenge on her behalf.'

'That's a possibility. She hasn't mentioned Lady Forbes-Chichester much, but perhaps that's the reason why. And why would she murder Mr Lawrence?'

'I don't know. I remember him laughing when she was telling us about the purchase of Nelson's Column.'

'Oh dear, poor Mrs Stanley-Piggot. I remember him

laughing, too. In fact, I think a few people mocked her for it. I suppose the only other person to consider is Lord Chichester.'

'Lord Chichester could have murdered his wife because there were difficulties in the marriage which we're yet to find out about,' said Lottie. 'And perhaps Mr Lawrence discovered some evidence that Lord Chichester murdered his wife and needed to be silenced.'

'Yes! That could be it! And one of these people we're discussing sent you that note, Lottie. They mentioned poison and Mr Lawrence was poisoned. It's very worrying!'

Chapter Forty-Eight

'OH DEAR, WILLIAM, WHAT'S HAPPENED?' said Lady Anna Forbes-Chichester as she arrived in the entrance hall of Hamilton Hall. Lord Chichester was leaning against a marble column and wiping his brow. He looked exhausted.

'Another murder,' he replied. 'What are you doing here, Anna?'

'I thought I'd call on you and see how you're holding up. But another murder? Who? How?'

'That awful Lawrence chap has been poisoned this afternoon.'

'Goodness.'

'And it turned out he stole most of his songs from someone else.'

'Really? Oh dear. I suppose his death has now saved him from the embarrassment of a very public downfall.'

'That's a good point, Anna. You don't suppose it was? No...'

'What?'

'Perhaps he did it deliberately?'

'What an awful thought.'

'He could have murdered Ruby because she threatened to tell everyone about the stolen songs. And then he poisoned himself when he got found out! That would tidy everything up nicely, wouldn't it? I shall tell the detective my theory. I'd say it's better than anything he's come up with.'

Anna looked up at the second Lady Chichester who was glaring at them from the wall. 'Shall we take a stroll, William?'

'Yes, I'd like that.'

They walked out to the terrace, and she took his arm. Her former husband seemed to have aged a great deal in the past few years. She felt sure that he wouldn't have aged quite so much if he had remained with her. The divorce case had taken its toll, and she suspected his second wife had been demanding, too. She'd been filled with youth and vigour whereas he'd reached the stage in life where he preferred a quiet day-to-day existence.

'I regret the divorce, you know,' she said. 'I acted impulsively. I know why I did it. I did it out of revenge. But really, when you consider how long we were married, there was no need for it. You were very silly indeed, but it would have blown over. These things always do. And then, before I knew it, you were marrying her. You would never have done that if I hadn't divorced you.'

'No, I wouldn't have done. And I suppose once the divorce case was underway, we found ourselves on a path from which there was no deviation. And when it was all finalised, I felt terribly sad about it. But Ruby was there, on my arm, giving me lots of attention. We all know why. She was desperate to be Lady Chichester, and she was desperate to live in this place. Who could blame her? I allowed her to do it. Very foolish of me. I have many regrets.'

Anna gripped his arm and wondered how desperate he'd been to leave his second marriage. Would he have resorted to murder?

'Obviously, I regret the decisions I've made,' he said. 'But that didn't mean I wanted my wife dead. Murdering people is never the answer to anything, you know, Anna.'

'You don't need to tell me that.'

'What do the children make of it now?'

'They're too busy with their own lives to care much, I'm afraid.'

'Oh dear. Is it really that bad? Have I pushed them away that much?'

'They never did approve. You know that, don't you?'

'Yes, I know that. I suppose I live in hope that, one day, I'll be forgiven.'

'Well, yes, they may do that. You just have to speak to them and find out.'

'We had such fun times together here, didn't we? When they were young. Running around the woods with the dogs. Paddling in the stream. The games of cricket we played on the lawn. All those long summer days. It was quite delightful, wasn't it?'

She felt a lump in her throat. 'Yes, it was. I miss those times. But time marches on. Even if we hadn't divorced, the children were always going to grow up and make lives for themselves, weren't they? You can't keep them here forever.'

'No. I suppose not. And maybe that's why I was so foolish. I suppose I realised I was getting older. I realised my children were growing up and that you and I, well... I suppose we were taking each other for granted at times. I've also realised now I needed to make more of an effort. But instead, I chose to pay attention to a young woman dancing on a stage. Well, I paid the price for that.'

'We both did, dear. But there's no use in being morose about it. We can't turn back the clock to those times. Instead, we must be grateful that we had those times together. And there's always hope for the future, you know.'

'Yes, there is.'

He stopped and turned to her. 'You didn't, by any chance...'

'What?'

He scratched his temple. 'On that evening. Did you sneak into the maze and...'

'No! I interrupted her performance, but that was all.'

'I see.'

Surely William could never suspect her of being a murderer? She wondered why he'd asked her the question. Was it to deflect suspicion from himself?

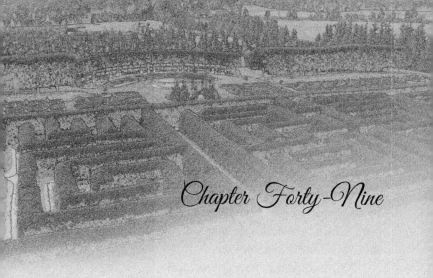

Chapter Forty-Nine

'Good golly, Lottie. Am I seeing things?' Mrs Moore picked up her lorgnette and peered out over the balcony. 'No, I'm not seeing things. Lord Chichester is walking arm-in-arm along the terrace with his first wife!'

Lottie followed her gaze and saw the pair deep in conversation.

'I wonder what they're talking about?' said Mrs Moore. 'I suppose she must be some comfort to him after everything that's happened. And... oh, goodness, Lottie. I've just had a thought!'

'What?'

'The pair of them could have been in it together!'

'Lady Chichester's murder, you mean?'

'Yes. They could have conspired to interrupt her performance and cause the chaos where all the guests ended up in the maze. Lord Chichester could then have suggested to his wife they rescue everyone, that's how he got her into the maze. And while she was distracted by Miss Darby, he did the deed!'

'But how did they know the guests would go into the maze? Surely they couldn't have planned for that?'

159

'That's a good question, Lottie. Maybe they just made a lucky assumption that they would. Anyway, I think the best thing to do is surprise them and see if they look guilty.'

Lottie didn't feel so sure about this. 'Really?'

'Yes.' Mrs Moore got up from her seat. 'Come along, Lottie. Let's see if we can find out what they're talking about.'

By the time they got down to the terrace, there was no sign of Lord Chichester or his former wife. A vivid orange sunset stretched along the western sky.

'Where could they have got to, Lottie?'

No sooner had Mrs Moore spoken than they spotted Lord Chichester walking towards them from the direction of the fountain.

'Good evening, ladies,' he said. 'You've come out to admire the beautiful sunset?'

Rosie trotted up to him and he greeted the corgi with a pat on the head.

'Yes, it's a beautiful sunset,' said Mrs Moore. 'I looked out of my window earlier and could tell it was going to be very pretty this evening. Perhaps I was mistaken, Lord Chichester, but I thought I saw you walking with a lady.'

'Ah yes, my first wife. She kindly paid me a visit to find out how I was faring. I had to tell her all about Lawrence keeling over after that dose of poison this afternoon. What a day!'

'Indeed it has been. Lady Forbes-Chichester has left now?'

'Yes, you've just missed her. She walked around the other side of the house back to her motor car.'

'Well, I think it's rather lovely you're on good terms with her after everything that's happened.'

'Yes.' He scratched his temple thoughtfully. 'It hasn't always been that way, but tragedy sometimes has a way of bringing people back together. I've been a bit of a fool, really.'

'What do you mean by that, Lord Chichester?'

'I'm not quite sure. But marriage can be a complicated business, can't it?'

'Absolutely. You're speaking to the right person, I've been married three times.'

'Have you really, Mrs Moore? I thought it was just the once.'

'No. Three times. My first husband died of rheumatic fever and my second husband died of drink. My third husband ran off with a dancer from Petoskey.'

'Peto... what?'

'It's a small town in Michigan. And then I had hopes of marrying Prince Manfred of Bavaria. But the better I got to know him, the more I went off him.'

'Ah yes. That can happen. I'm sorry to hear you've been unlucky in love.'

'It seems it happens to many of us. Apart from Mrs Stanley-Piggot, I suppose. She told us she was married for over thirty-three years and that she and her husband were blissfully happy.'

'Blissfully happy?' said Lord Chichester. 'Presumably that's how she likes to think of it now. I knew her husband Francis well and let's just say he had a roving eye.'

'Oh dear. Really?'

'She must have known about it. Perhaps she didn't? Anyway, I suppose it's quite nice she thinks so fondly of him after his death.' He checked his watch. 'I think I have to speak to the detective again shortly. He's got his work cut out now after Mr Lawrence's demise. In fact, I have a theory about that.'

'Is that so?'

'Yes.' Lord Chichester glanced around, then lowered his voice. 'I think he murdered my wife because he didn't want her telling anyone about the stolen songs. And then I think he poisoned himself because he couldn't face the shame of being found out!'

'Golly. That's quite a theory, Lord Chichester.'

Lottie felt a pang of guilt. Could Quentin Lawrence have poisoned himself because she helped reveal his secret?

'Anyway, I'm going to see if the detective has finished speaking to Miss Darby yet. And then I'm going to put it to him!'

Lord Chichester went back into the house.

'It will be interesting to know what the detective makes of his theory, Lottie,' said Mrs Moore. 'Do you think he could be onto something? Or is he suggesting it so no one suspects him and Lady Forbes-Chichester?'

DAISY DARBY FOLDED her arms and glared at Detective Inspector Wilson. 'I had nothing to do with these murders!'

'But you were in close proximity to both victims at the time of their deaths. How do you explain that?'

'Bad luck!'

'Bad luck? Is that your only explanation?'

'What other explanation do you want? I'm not the murderer. You need to be looking for someone else.'

'Let's go through the facts again, shall we, Miss Darby? You happened to be standing with Lady Chichester in the maze the other evening when an arm appeared through a hedge and stabbed her.'

'Yes. That's what happened.'

'You do realise that we only have your word for it?'

'Yes, I do, Detective. But I know what I saw. And besides, Lady Chichester was facing me while I was speaking to her. How could I possibly stab her from behind?'

'Perhaps the attack didn't happen while you were speaking to her. Perhaps you finished your conversation, she turned away from you, and that's when you attacked her.'

'No, Detective, that's not what happened! And besides, she would have fought back. I wouldn't have been able to get away with it.'

'And now we have Quentin Lawrence, his cup of tea poisoned. You served the tea, Miss Darby.'

'I didn't put poison in it!'

'And you were sitting close to him when he was poisoned.'

'Everyone was! We were all sitting around that coffee table. It could have been anyone.'

The detective sat back in his chair and sighed. He turned to the sergeant. 'Can I see what you've written please, Travers?'

The sergeant handed him the notebook. He flicked through it and gave another sigh.

Daisy suspected he was lost for ideas.

'Can you see the difficulty I have here, Miss Darby? It's a struggle to believe someone would thrust a knife through a hedge. And it's also difficult to believe someone could so blatantly put poison in a cup of tea while it's sitting in front of everyone on a coffee table.'

'I understand it's difficult to believe, Detective, but it's what happened. I'm trying to be helpful! I've told you what I saw. This murderer is clearly very clever.'

'I think you must have put the poison into Mr Lawrence's cup when you poured out the tea.'

'I didn't!'

'And when he collapsed and the drawing room descended into chaos, you put your box of rat poison into the ming vase.'

'Impossible!'

'And out of the guests staying here, you're the only one who can be closely linked to both Lady Chichester and Quentin Lawrence. You were envious of Lady Chichester and you wanted to leave the Pom-Pom Duo. It made sense to you to get rid of them both.'

'It makes no sense at all!'

Daisy was worried. How else could she defend herself? Whatever she said, the detective seemed determined not to listen.

She wished she could appear more upset about their deaths. The truth was, she'd been annoyed with both of them. And with them both gone, she had the freedom to do what she liked.

Hopefully that included marrying Lord Moorcroft and becoming Lady Moorcroft of Mansfield Grange.

It was proving difficult to plead her innocence, and it was difficult to do so when she realised she was now better off.

'Are you smiling, Miss Darby?' asked the detective.

She checked herself, realising her thoughts were showing on her face.

'No,' she said.

'I'm sure I saw a smile playing on your lips just then. I find your behaviour most unusual, Miss Darby.'

'Detective, I don't think anybody can predict how they're going to react when they've been accused of two murders. This is an extremely difficult time, and all sorts of thoughts are racing through my mind. I'm sorry if I don't appear to be in full control of my emotions.'

She gave a little whimper and dried an imaginary tear from her eye.

The detective's eyes narrowed. 'I'm afraid you're not being very convincing, Miss Darby.'

Chapter Fifty-One

'MISS DARBY HAS BEEN in the morning room with the detective for ages,' said Mrs Moore. 'What can they possibly be discussing?'

'She has to be the murderer,' said Margaret Stanley-Piggot.

'Definitely,' said Maria Lawrence. 'She murdered Lady Chichester and my husband. The detective should arrest her and march her down to the police station!'

They all sat in the sitting room. The clock said it was almost ten and Rosie dozed by Lottie's feet.

'Yes, she should be arrested this evening,' said Mrs Stanley-Piggot. 'Then we can all get a good night's sleep tonight and go home tomorrow.'

'Goodness, it's going to be very strange at home without Quentin,' said Mrs Lawrence. 'I can't even imagine it.'

'I'm so sorry, Mrs Lawrence,' said Mrs Moore. 'It must be very difficult for you.'

'I don't think it's quite sunk in yet,' said Mrs Lawrence. 'And all that business about the stolen songs... I knew nothing about it! How did Lady Chichester know about it and I didn't? It makes me wonder what else he hid from me. In fact,

I don't want to know. You think you know someone and then you find out all these awful things...'

The door opened and Daisy Darby walked in. Everyone fell silent. She gave them all a smile and sat herself in an easy chair.

'You can carry on your conversation,' she said.

Mrs Lawrence gave a sniff. 'No, we can't. Not with you in the room. You murdered my husband, Miss Darby!'

She got up from her chair and swept out of the room.

Chapter Fifty-Two

DAISY DARBY WENT UP to her room. She didn't want to spend a moment longer in anyone else's company.

Everyone seemed convinced she was the murderer.

She opened the doors of her balcony and stepped out. Somewhere in the darkness below lay the maze.

A cursed labyrinth.

She wished she had never set foot in it.

What would tomorrow bring? She couldn't bear the thought of everyone talking about her and accusing her of murder.

It would be better if she left this horrible place. She could pack her things into her case, leave via the garden and flag a motor car down on the road. She could find a hotel in a nearby town and get a train back to London in the morning.

What a perfect idea. Why hadn't she done it sooner?

She turned to go back into her room and pack her case.

But someone blocked her way.

She glared at them. 'What on earth are *you* doing here?'

Chapter Fifty-Three

DETECTIVE INSPECTOR WILSON looked bereft as everyone gathered in the sitting room. The clock said it was almost eleven.

'I've never known a case like it,' he said. 'A lady who I was speaking to a little over an hour ago is now dead!'

Lottie, Mrs Moore, Lord Chichester, Mrs Stanley-Piggot and Mrs Lawrence sat in stunned silence. Sally the maid was also in the room. Her hands fidgeted nervously.

'Now we've ascertained that everyone had retired to their bedrooms at the time of Miss Darcy's fall from her balcony at half-past ten. Please tell me again what you heard, Sally,' said the detective.

'I was just closing the window, sir, before I got into bed. And I heard someone shout "help!"'

'And you think it was Miss Darby who said that?'

'Yes, it sounded like her.'

'And to be clear, your room is two storeys directly above Miss Darby's balcony?'

'Yes.'

'Did you hear anything else?'

'Nothing else, sir.'

'So you didn't hear the other person speak?'

'No, sir.'

'Thank you, Sally.'

Lord Chichester cleared his throat. 'Is it possible that Miss Darby jumped, Detective?'

'In which case, why would she cry out "help"?'

'I don't know. But this may not be murder. And I've already mentioned to you that Mr Lawrence's death may not be murder either.'

'I can't find any reason why either of them would do such a thing deliberately,' said the detective. 'It doesn't make sense.'

'Quentin Lawrence wanted to avoid shame and Daisy Darby wanted to avoid being arrested for the murder of my wife. The net was closing in on her, so she found a way out.'

The detective sighed. 'I don't believe Miss Darby would have shouted the word "help" if she'd purposefully jumped off her balcony.'

'Perhaps young Sally is mistaken?' said Lord Chichester.

The detective turned to the maid. 'Do you think you're mistaken, Sally?'

She shook her head. 'No. I know what I heard.'

'Very well,' said the detective. 'You all look too shocked and tired to be of any more use this evening. I think everyone needs to get some rest and I shall speak with all of you in the morning. And please try your hardest not to get murdered tonight.'

Chapter Fifty-Four

'THANK goodness we're all still alive,' said Mrs Moore at breakfast the following morning.

'I didn't sleep a wink,' said Mrs Stanley-Piggot.

'Me neither,' said Mrs Lawrence.

Lottie had barely slept either. She passed a piece of bacon to Rosie beneath the table.

She had lain awake during the night wondering who the murderer could be. She had tried to recall every observation and conversation from the previous few days. She had a good memory for detail, but how could she decide what was relevant and what wasn't?

After breakfast, she and Mrs Moore spoke to Detective Inspector Wilson, who looked more tired than anyone else.

'I think the man is almost ready to give up,' said Mrs Moore after they left the morning room. 'We weren't able to help him with anything, were we? And you usually get some good ideas about things like this, Lottie, but I think this case has just about beaten you too, hasn't it?'

'Possibly,' said Lottie. 'But I'm still going over everything in my mind. I'm deciding what's important and what isn't. I keep thinking about the fact you accidentally picked up Mrs Stanley-Piggot's tea yesterday. The cups were quite muddled on that table.'

'They were. Odd of you to remember a little detail like that, though.'

'It's got me thinking. Perhaps Quentin Lawrence picked up the wrong cup?'

'You think the poisoned tea wasn't intended for him?'

'I don't know yet. I need to do some more thinking.'

'Well, why don't you do it on a little walk. I'd like to do that stroll by the river again. I don't much like being in this house. Do you?'

'Not really.'

A short while later, Lottie, Mrs Moore and Rosie walked down the driveway.

'Another lovely day, Lottie.' Mrs Moore breathed in the air. 'Even when something terrible happens, the sun still manages to shine, doesn't it? The birds sing in the trees and life goes on.'

They reached the workers' cottages and turned right.

'There's Nellie Harrison again,' said Lottie. The old, stooped woman watched them from her gate.

To Lottie's surprise, Rosie scampered over to greet her. The old lady opened the gate and bent down to say hello to the corgi.

As they walked over to the old lady, her niece, Rosamund, stepped out of the cottage. 'Hello again!' she said. 'It's nice to see you, Mrs Moore and Miss Sprigg.'

'That's very kind of you to remember our names.'

'Well, Auntie Nellie and I always remember the names of people who are kind to us. Unfortunately, few people are. Auntie Nellie is often dismissed as a mad lady just because people find conversation with her difficult. She's not easy, but a kind word or gesture isn't too much to ask, is it?'

'No, it's not at all.'

'The trouble is, most people around here don't have the decency to do that. Even some of the guests at the house this weekend.'

Mrs Moore rolled her eyes. 'Well, yes, there are some interesting characters there.'

'You'd think his lord and her ladyship would have shown some kindness, but no. It's the way they are. I'm sorry, I should watch what I'm saying. I realise that the death of Lady Chichester is extremely tragic and Lord Chichester must be enormously upset. I'm sure the detective is working very hard on it. Because when something like that happens to someone who's wealthy and grand, these cases get solved quickly, don't they?'

'Perhaps, although this case is proving complicated.'

'Naughty Tommy,' said Nellie.

'Who is Tommy?' Mrs Moore asked her.

'Naughty Tommy Brewster. He was a thief.'

'Brewster?' said Rosamund. 'I'd forgotten his surname. I haven't heard you mention it for a long time.'

'So Tommy Brewster was a thief and he once lived on the estate?' said Lottie.

'Yes,' said Rosamund. 'Sometimes Auntie tells us more details, but I'm afraid I don't remember much more than that. Didn't you once say he had a shovel, Auntie?'

'Yes. I saw Tommy Brewster with a shovel.'

'Well, I think it's time you came inside for a cup of tea.' Rosamund turned to Lottie and Mrs Moore. 'Would you like to join us? Our house isn't as grand as Hamilton Hall, but I've just baked some biscuits.'

'Biscuits?' said Mrs Moore. 'That sounds perfect!'

Chapter Fifty-Five

'WELL, that turned out to be an extremely interesting half an hour,' said Mrs Moore as they left Rosamund and Nellie's cottage. 'What do we do now?'

'Look for evidence,' said Lottie.

'Do you think you can find some?'

'Yes, but it's probably hidden.'

They paused on the driveway and surveyed the vast frontage of Hamilton Hall.

'It could be like looking for a needle in a haystack, Lottie.'

'If you lived in a house like this and wanted to hide some old documents, Mrs Moore, where would you put them?'

'I suppose the attic would be the obvious place. But how on earth are you going to get in there, Lottie?'

'I know someone who can help.'

* * *

'You want to go into the attic?' said Sally. 'Why?' She was carrying a basket of neatly folded laundry.

'I think it will help me solve these murders.'

Sally's eyes widened. 'Really?'

'There might be some useful documents up there.'

'I'm not sure I like the idea of going behind Lord Chichester's back.'

'I can understand that.' Lottie quickly explained to Sally the cases she'd been involved with in the past. 'I can't promise I can solve this case. But I'd like to try,' she added.

Sally smiled. 'I'm impressed. Perhaps you're a very good storyteller, Miss Sprigg, but I choose to believe you. I'll fetch the key. Meet me on the top floor in a few minutes.'

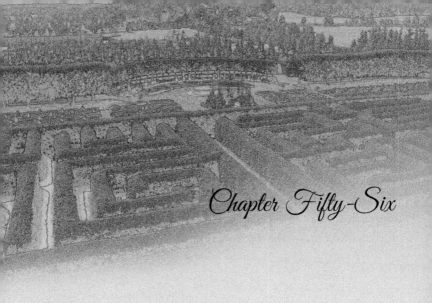

SALLY, Lottie and Rosie met on the top floor where the servants' bedrooms were. Sally led them to a narrow door at the end of the corridor and glanced around her to check there was no one about. Then she took a key from her apron pocket and unlocked the door. She opened it and Lottie winced as the hinges gave a squeak.

'Here, you'll need this.' Sally handed Lottie a torch. 'I'll also give you the key so you can lock the door from the inside. You don't want anybody walking in and discovering you up there. I would come with you, but it's a bit spooky, to be honest with you.'

'Thank you, Sally. I'm very grateful.'

'You'd better go now before anyone notices. Good luck.'

Lottie stepped through the door. The darkness which lay beyond it meant Rosie was reluctant to follow.

'It will be alright, Rosie.' Lottie picked her up and carried her through. Then she turned on her torch, shut the door behind her and locked it. Ahead of her, she could see an old, steep staircase of wooden slats. Cautiously, Lottie climbed it with Rosie under one arm. It wasn't easy as she tried to hold the torch as well.

When she reached the top of the staircase, she swung the torch beam around her and was astonished by the size of the space. The eaves were steeply pitched and supported by large, old timbers. The air was musty. Around her sat old chests, crates, boxes and pieces of furniture. Everything that was no longer needed in the main part of the house had clearly been put here over the years.

The floorboards were a little uneven, and she reminded herself to tread carefully so she didn't trip and make a noise. She placed Rosie down, and the dog remained close by her as she carefully made her way around the attic, stepping quietly so no one in a room beneath would hear her footsteps.

Spider webs heavy with dust hung from the rafters. Lottie hoped she wouldn't come across any large spiders up here. Or rats, for that matter.

'From what Nellie and Rosamund said, we need to look for something that's been up here for a while,' Lottie whispered to Rosie. 'About twenty to thirty years. Some of these boxes have been put here recently.'

Many items seemed quite new to the attic, they had little dust on them. Lottie imagined the second Lady Chichester clearing them out from the house when she married. She probably hadn't wanted too many reminders of her husband's first marriage around her.

Lottie began cautiously lifting the lids of boxes and chests. She found old clothes, books and ornaments, but no papers.

Lottie's torch beam picked out a painting. It showed a man of about seventy. He wore smart, Victorian clothing and was standing with a spaniel. 'I think he must be the previous Lord Chichester,' whispered Lottie.

Close to the portrait was a large wooden chest which looked

as though it had been in the attic for some time. Lottie put her torch in her pocket and placed her fingers beneath the lid. It had clearly been shut for a long time and required some effort to open it. Eventually, she was able to lift it up. She reached for her torch and was just about to shine it inside when she heard a noise.

She held her breath.

Then she heard the noise again. It sounded like a key in a lock. And then the creaking sound of the attic door hinges.

Chapter Fifty-Seven

Was it Sally entering the attic? Maybe she was coming to tell Lottie something. But when Lottie heard the footsteps on the wooden slats, they were slow and heavy. They didn't seem to belong to the maid.

Carefully, Lottie lowered the lid of the chest.

'Rosie!' she whispered. 'We've got to hide somewhere!'

Rosie's tail began to wag. She was clearly keen to meet the person who was making their way up the staircase.

'Come on!' Lottie gripped Rosie's collar and led her behind the large chest. It didn't quite shield the pair of them, but there wasn't enough time to find a better place.

Lottie turned off her torch and crouched down, making herself as small as possible. She huddled Rosie next to her and prayed the dog wouldn't bark and give them away.

The visitor reached the top of the staircase and the beam of their torch swept across the attic like a searchlight. Had they heard Lottie up here?

Lottie bowed her head even more and tried to breathe as silently as possible.

The footsteps progressed through the attic. Heavy and slow.

As they drew nearer, Lottie prayed Rosie would keep quiet and still. Her heart pounded so heavily, she felt sure the visitor could hear it.

Then the footsteps stopped by the chest. Lottie clenched her teeth. The other person was only four or five feet away from her.

She screwed her eyes shut. All she had to do was hang on to this moment and be as quiet as possible. She felt Rosie shift a little. Would the visitor detect it? If they shone their torch beyond the chest, then Lottie felt sure she and Rosie would be spotted.

Eventually, the footsteps moved on. Lottie breathed a little easier, but she knew she was still in danger.

She opened her eyes and saw the torchlight further along the attic now. Now and again she caught sight of the visitor's silhouette in front of the beam.

It looked like Lord Chichester.

She could feel a tickle at the back of her throat, as if the dust in the air had irritated it. She felt as though she were going to cough or sneeze and she could only hope she would do neither. She put a hand over her nose and mouth, desperately trying to stop herself. Eventually, the sensation subsided.

Lord Chichester trained his torch on a box in front of him. Then he stooped down and opened it.

'Aha,' she heard him say.

Lottie relaxed a little further. He had come up to the attic to look for something else. He wasn't looking for her. But she knew that the slightest noise from her or Rosie would alert him to their presence. She still had to be extremely careful.

Lord Chichester was looking in the box for something. The sound of him rummaging about filled the attic. Then he lifted out a large book and rested it on another box next to him. Slowly, he began to turn its thick pages.

Lottie wondered what the book was. And how long was Lord Chichester going to spend up here? Her legs were squashed so much that they were hurting. And Rosie was growing restless.

Why was Lord Chichester here? If he was looking for something, then why hadn't he asked a member of his staff to fetch it for him? She could only imagine the item he was looking at was personal to him.

Was it possible he'd come up here to hide something? Her mind raced with thoughts and ideas. But most of all, she felt desperate for him to leave again. She needed to change position to ease the discomfort, but she knew she couldn't risk moving at all.

Lottie couldn't believe how well Rosie was behaving, although she knew that could change at any moment. Especially if Lord Chichester did something to startle the dog.

She watched him take something from the book and tuck it into his jacket pocket. Then he placed the book back into the box and closed it again. He straightened himself and Lottie ducked lower as he made his way past her again and headed in the direction of the staircase. She hoped he was leaving now and that he wouldn't occupy himself with something else up here in the attic.

When she heard his footsteps on the staircase, she felt relieved she would soon be safe to look around the attic again. But she didn't move until she heard the door open, then close again and the key turn in the lock.

'Thank goodness for that, Rosie,' she whispered. She waited a moment just in case Lord Chichester changed his mind and returned. Then she slowly stretched herself out. Her legs felt numb below her knees and she had tensed up so much that her shoulders felt they were stuck beneath her ears.

Cautiously, she turned the torch back on and felt the sharp tingle of blood returning to her legs.

'Let's go and see what he was looking at,' she whispered.

She stepped over to the box Lord Chichester had opened and shone her torch on it. Then, she lifted the lid just as he had done. Several large books were stacked inside.

'Photograph albums,' she said to Rosie.

The photograph album on top was clearly special. It was covered with cream silk and decorated with lace. As she lifted the cover, she saw it was an album of wedding photographs.

They weren't photographs of Lord Chichester's recent wedding. Instead, they were photographs of his first wedding. A slim, youthful Lord Chichester stood arm-in-arm with his beautiful bride who wore the longest bridal train Lottie had ever seen.

Had Lord Chichester's recent meeting with his former wife prompted him to look at this album? And was the item he'd put in his pocket a photograph?

Lottie turned the page. There were no photographs on this one, instead some pressed flowers had been glued to the page. They were presumably from the bridal bouquet. There was something rather sad about the faded pink roses.

Then Lottie remembered something about a rose.

'Perhaps I'm mistaken, Rosie?'

Her words meant nothing to the dog. And she wasn't sure what they meant to her, either.

She closed the album and the box and went back to the large chest she had been about to open before Lord Chichester arrived.

She opened it to see bundles of paper tied up with string.

'This is what I came for,' she said. 'Let's hope this doesn't take long, Rosie.'

ONCE SHE'D FINISHED in the attic, Lottie brushed off the cobwebs from her clothes, returned the key to Sally, made her way to the morning room with Rosie, and knocked at the door.

'Come in!' came Detective Inspector Wilson's voice from within.

Lottie stepped into the room to see Margaret Stanley-Piggot sitting with the detective and sergeant.

'Oh, I'm sorry,' said Lottie. 'I didn't mean to interrupt.'

'We were just finishing,' said the weary-looking detective.

'Good,' said Mrs Stanley-Piggot, getting to her feet. 'Can I go home now?'

'Not just yet, I'm afraid.'

'But I really must get home, I have a pressing engagement! You can't keep us all here forever, Detective!'

'I shall address you all shortly, Mrs Stanley-Piggot.' He turned to Lottie. 'I'm assuming your interruption means you have some important information, Miss Sprigg?'

'Yes.'

Mrs Stanley-Piggot left the room and Lottie sat in the seat she'd just left.

'Well?'

Lottie cleared her throat as she realised how silly her accusation was going to sound. 'I believe Lord Chichester is a fraud, sir.'

He narrowed his eyes. 'A fraud?'

'Yes. I don't think he inherited this estate. I think he stole it.'

The detective gave a laugh. 'How can someone possibly steal an estate?'

'With fraudulent papers.'

'I see.' He sat back in his chair to listen. 'Go on.'

'At the anniversary party, Lord Chichester gave a speech, and he told everyone his life story. It seemed an odd thing to do, and I wondered at the time why he did it. I realise now that he wanted everyone to believe it.'

'It's fair to say some people like to control what others think about them. But Lord Chichester?'

'Yes, and then Mrs Moore and I met Nellie Harrison.'

'Oh dear.' Detective Inspector Wilson leant forward again. 'The local mad lady.'

'She said Tommy Brewster was a thief.'

'Yes, she's been saying that for many years.'

'Have you ever wondered why?'

'Because she's mad.'

'Do you know who Tommy Brewster is?'

'No.'

'Well, her niece seems to think he was once a worker on this estate. Nellie apparently recalls seeing him with a shovel. When Mrs Moore and I met her this morning, she told us Tommy was a lord.'

'Nellie Harrison is not a reliable source of information, Miss Sprigg. If this is the best you've got, then I'm afraid—'

'I found some papers in the attic just now,' said Lottie. 'There's a neatly drawn-up will naming William Chichester as the beneficiary.'

'There you go.'

'But it could be forged. And I can't find any other paperwork which supports the existence of someone called William Chichester.'

'That doesn't mean it doesn't exist, Miss Sprigg. Are you trying to make something of a mad lady's crazy theory?'

'I did find some papers belonging to Tommy Brewster.'

'What?'

'Just a few. I think he probably disposed of most of them, but he'd kept these because they appeared to be letters from a sweetheart in London. They're addressed to Tommy Brewster at Hamilton Hall and he appears to have been working here as a gardener thirty years ago. You can read them yourself, Detective. There's quite a bundle of them. I left them in the chest in the attic.'

'I see.' He pulled at his tie. 'So you're saying Lord Chichester is actually Tommy Brewster, and he fraudulently inherited this estate?'

'Yes.'

'I shall have to look into this, you know.'

'I understand that, Detective.'

'And if it's true, then Lord Chichester has been sitting on an enormous secret.'

'He must have been willing to go to great lengths to protect his secret, sir,' said Sergeant Travers.

'Yes indeed.' The detective gave this some thought. 'I wonder if the late Lady Chichester discovered his identity.' He turned to Lottie. 'Are you suggesting Lord Chichester is the murderer, Miss Sprigg?'

'No.'

'No?'

185

'I thought he was before I went into the attic, but I now realise it's someone else.'

'Who?'

Chapter Fifty-Nine

DETECTIVE INSPECTOR WILSON dashed out of the room as soon as Lottie told him.

'Where's Mrs Stanley-Piggot got to?' he called out. 'She was here a few minutes ago!'

Lottie recalled how keen Mrs Stanley-Piggot had been to get home. Was it possible she'd left already?

Lottie followed the detective out of the room. They encountered Lord Chichester in the corridor.

'What's going on?' he said.

'She's a suspect,' said the detective. 'And I've got some urgent questions for her, Mr Brewster.'

'What did you just call me?' Lord Chichester's face paled, and he staggered back against the wall.

The detective marched on and ordered a search of the house for Mrs Stanley-Piggot.

Lottie found Mrs Moore and Mrs Lawrence in the sitting room.

'Goodness, Lottie, what's all this palaver about?'

'The detective needs to speak to Mrs Stanley-Piggot, but I think she's run off.'

'Run off?' Mrs Moore got to her feet. 'She can't have got far.'

'We'll find her!' said Mrs Lawrence.

Everyone searched Hamilton Hall. Lottie bumped into Sally in the drawing room. 'I've checked the bedrooms,' said the maid. 'Including Mrs Stanley-Piggot's room. All her belongings are still there. I don't think she'd have gone far without them, would she?'

'No, I don't think she would,' said Lottie. 'She has to be hiding somewhere nearby.' Her eye was drawn to the maze beyond the window. 'I wonder?'

Chapter Sixty

LOTTIE RAN upstairs to her bedroom to fetch her ball of string. She didn't want to enter the maze without it.

Rosie cantered after her as she ran. Moments later, they were outside on the terrace.

Lots of people were searching the house for Mrs Stanley-Piggot, but she hadn't seen anyone go into the maze to look for her.

Lottie tied the end of her string firmly to a yew branch at the entrance of the maze and went in.

She listened out for the sound of a foot tread but couldn't hear anything. The ball of string unwound as she and Rosie quietly made their way along the path.

As she walked, Lottie realised she was in a risky situation. Lady Chichester had died from a knife being thrust through a hedge. Was she foolish to come here?

She moved as quietly as she could, listening carefully for any noise from the paths beyond the hedges around her. Once again, it was silent in here. None of the paths looked familiar, even though this was the third time Lottie had come here.

She reached a few dead ends and had to go back on herself.

She felt disorientated, but she had the string to help her. As time passed, she grew hopeful there was no one else in the maze with her. Perhaps Mrs Stanley-Piggot was hiding elsewhere.

When Lottie found the centre of the maze, she wondered how many of the paths she had covered. And was it a good use of her time being here? For all she knew, Detective Inspector Wilson had now apprehended Mrs Stanley-Piggot in the house and was waiting for Lottie to give him an explanation.

After a few more minutes, she considered giving up her search and retracing her way back to the entrance.

'I don't think we're in the right place, Rosie.'

Something dropped near her feet.

Lottie startled. It was a stone.

Had someone just thrown a stone at her?

She turned to see another ball of string a few yards away on the path behind her.

'Someone's followed us and wound up the string!' she said to Rosie.

Then a laugh rang out from the other side of the hedge.

'Stop right there!' Lottie called out.

She picked up the other ball of string and ran towards the direction of the laughter. Then Rosie took off ahead of her.

'Rosie! Wait!'

The dog was too fast for her and soon Lottie was lost.

'Rosie!'

Her dog was somewhere in the maze. And so was Mrs Stanley-Piggot.

All Lottie could do was run and hope she'd find Rosie. Had Rosie found Mrs Stanley-Piggot?

Lottie found the exit to the maze.

But where was Rosie?

Mrs Moore and Detective Inspector Wilson rushed out onto the terrace.

'Are you alright, Lottie?'

'No! Rosie's run after Mrs Stanley-Piggot and I can't find either of them!'

'We heard a shout,' said the detective. 'That's why we came running out. Mrs Stanley-Piggot is in the maze?'

'Yes. She threw a stone at me.'

'Are you hurt?' said Mrs Moore.

'She missed. But I'm worried about Rosie!'

'I'll go in,' said the detective. 'Wait here.'

Lottie felt a cold lurch in her stomach. 'Mrs Stanley-Piggot has murdered three people!' she said. 'Surely that means she'd also harm a dog?'

'She's the murderer?' said Mrs Moore. 'I thought it was Lord Chichester.'

'So did I, but then I changed my mind.'

'Oh golly, poor Rosie. Hopefully she'll bite her.'

'I hope so too.'

'Wait! I can hear something.'

They fell silent, and Lottie strained her ears to listen.

There was an unmistakable growling noise.

'I don't think it's coming from the maze,' said Lottie. 'I think they're in the garden.'

She ran around the perimeter of the maze to where the gap was. She could hear Mrs Moore puffing behind her.

As Lottie rounded the corner, she saw Mrs Stanley-Piggot staggering on the lawn at the back of the maze.

'Get off me, you brute!' she shouted.

But Rosie wasn't letting go. She growled as she clung on to Mrs Stanley-Piggot's skirts.

'Hooray!' puffed Mrs Moore. 'Rosie stopped her!'

'RIGHT THEN, MISS SPRIGG,' said Detective Inspector Wilson. 'You'd better have a good explanation for causing this drama this morning.'

Everyone was in the sitting room. Mrs Stanley-Piggot sat in a chair next to Sergeant Travers. She was sneering at Lottie. Lord Chichester sat alone, still looking pale.

Mrs Lawrence shared the sofa with Lottie and Mrs Moore. The detective paced the room near the door so Mrs Stanley-Piggot couldn't make her escape.

'It was a rose which made me remember something,' said Lottie.

'You'll need to explain yourself better than that,' said the detective.

Lottie took in a breath and tried to explain herself clearly. 'We know the person who murdered Lady Chichester was wearing gloves because they left no prints on the knife. So they either put on some gloves in order to commit the crime, or they were already wearing them. All the ladies who attended the party were wearing evening gloves.'

'That's right,' said Mrs Moore. 'I was wearing a pair of gloves myself.'

'As was I,' said Mrs Lawrence. 'We all were. That makes it almost impossible for you to work out who could have been holding the knife.'

'I don't see how you can tell it was me,' said Mrs Stanley-Piggot.

'After the murder, you pricked your finger on the floral arrangement in the ballroom,' said Lottie. 'You commented that the beautiful decorations were now wasted and you touched a rose in the display.'

'Yes, I did. But I don't see what that has to do with anything.'

'I can recall now that you weren't wearing your gloves,' said Lottie. 'If you had been, the prick to your finger wouldn't have hurt so much and you wouldn't have put your finger in your mouth.'

Mrs Stanley-Piggot laughed. 'And that makes me a murderer?'

'I thought little of it at the time. But when I look back, I recall you were wearing evening gloves, just like all the other ladies. At some point, you removed those gloves. I think you removed them because you damaged a glove when you attacked Lady Chichester.'

'Ridiculous.'

'Let me explain a bit more,' said Lottie. 'You were wearing sapphire blue gloves that evening, and they matched your gown. When you positioned yourself on the other side of the hedge from where Miss Darby and Lady Chichester were having their conversation, you heard their voices and took your opportunity. That was probably when you took the knife from your handbag, and then you thrust your arm through the hedge and stabbed Lady Chichester. I suspect the action of doing that and pulling your arm out of the hedge again probably snagged the delicate fabric of your gloves. You didn't want anyone to see that you had damaged them, so you took them off and put them in your handbag.'

'This is ridiculous!' said Mrs Stanley-Piggot.

'So what happened to your gloves?' asked Mrs Lawrence.

'I took them off, that was true. But I only did so because they kept slipping down, anyway. They were very annoying gloves, and I was quite pleased to have removed them and put them in my bag.'

'Presumably, the gloves are still in your possession, Mrs Stanley-Piggot?' asked the detective.

'Probably, I don't know.'

'So, if what Miss Sprigg is saying is correct, one of those gloves would have been damaged from the hedge.'

'I wouldn't know. I didn't put my arm through the hedge. They were very delicate gloves so they may well have got snagged on something else.'

'Travers,' said Detective Inspector Wilson. 'Please search the lady's room for the gloves.'

Mrs Stanley-Piggot bit her lip as the sergeant left the room.

'Now then, Miss Sprigg,' said the detective. 'Are you saying that Mrs Stanley-Piggot then poisoned Mr Lawrence and pushed Daisy Darby off the balcony?'

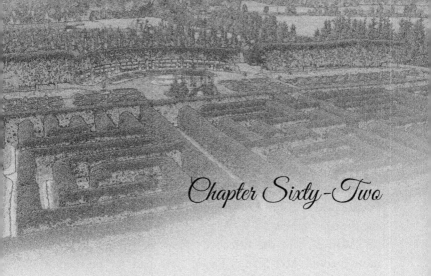

Chapter Sixty-Two

'I THINK Mrs Stanley-Piggot came to the event this weekend intent on murder,' said Lottie. 'She brought a knife with her and also obtained poison.'

'And where would I get the poison from?'

'I spoke to Sally the maid while she was checking the bedrooms for signs of mice,' said Lottie. 'The housekeeper had told her one of the guests had reported mice in their room, but Sally couldn't find any evidence of anything. I think that guest could have been Mrs Stanley-Piggot. I think she probably convinced a servant to fetch some rat poison for her.'

'You can't prove that was me!' said Mrs Stanley-Piggot.

'But the housekeeper might remember,' said the detective. 'I'll ring for her.'

He stepped over to the servant bell and pressed it.

Mrs Stanley-Piggot's confidence seemed to leave her, and she bit her lip again.

'Even if I did ask for some rat poison,' she said. 'I couldn't have possibly got away with putting it in the tea.'

'We were all sat around the coffee table,' said Lottie. 'Most of our cups were within each other's reach and we were distracted by the conversation about Mr Lawrence's theft of the songbook.'

'It was a risky move,' said the detective. 'But you carried it off, Mrs Stanley-Piggot.'

'I didn't do it!'

'And Miss Darby's murder?' said the detective.

'The only suspects by this point could have been Mrs Lawrence, Lord Chichester and Mrs Stanley-Piggot,' said Lottie. 'And out of those three, I think Mrs Stanley-Piggot had the strongest motive.'

'Motive!' said the detective. 'Now we get to it! What motive could Mrs Stanley-Piggot have had for murdering Daisy Darby?'

'Her late husband, Francis.'

'Leave him out of this!' shouted Mrs Stanley-Piggot.

'I think something happened between him and Daisy Darby,' said Lottie. 'Mrs Lawrence told Mrs Moore and me that she'd warned Miss Darby about going after wealthy married men.'

'That's true,' said Mrs Lawrence. 'I did.'

'Mrs Stanley-Piggot made no secret of her disapproval of Lord Chichester's second marriage,' said Lottie. 'The thought of a young woman luring a man away from his wife clearly bothered her.'

'I'd say it bothers most people!' said Mrs Stanley-Piggot.

'And then you and Lord Chichester contradicted each other. You told me and Mrs Moore that you'd been happily married for over thirty-three years. Lord Chichester told us, however, that your husband had a roving eye.'

Mrs Stanley-Piggot turned on Lord Chichester. 'You said *what*, William?'

Lord Chichester gave a resigned shrug. He had remained sullen since the detective had called him Mr Brewster earlier.

'Is it true?' asked the detective.

'Francis was a very dear friend of mine,' said Lord Chichester. 'And he was also absurdly rich. Some ladies were drawn to that and I suppose he was not entirely indifferent to their attentions.'

Mrs Stanley-Piggot gave a sniff.

'Were you really happily married for over thirty-three years, Mrs Stanley-Piggot?'

'We were married for thirty-three years, four months and seventeen days. And after he died...'

She stopped and her gaze dropped to the floor.

The room was silent.

'After Francis died...' she continued. 'I found love letters from her!'

'Who?' asked the detective.

'Daisy Darby! Who else?'

'And your act of revenge was to push her off her balcony?'

Lottie thought for a moment she would confess. But then her face twisted into a sneer. 'No!'

Sergeant Travers returned to the room with a pair of sapphire blue gloves in his hand. He handed them to the detective who inspected them.

'Were these the gloves you wore on the evening of Lady Chichester's murder, Mrs Stanley-Piggot?' asked the detective.

'I can't remember.'

'These are indeed delicate gloves. There are a few wine stains on them and a few snags here and there. They're not particularly robust. But they're useful enough for keeping one's fingerprints off something. And if I look at the arm of this right-hand glove here, the snags and tears to the material are quite visible. I'd say this glove could have been on an arm which was shoved through a hedge.'

The housekeeper entered the room. 'How can I help?' She was an austere lady in a long black dress.

'We believe one of the guests reported mice in their room,' said the detective. 'Could you please tell us who it was?'

'Yes, it was Mrs Stanley-Piggot.'

'Did you find mice in her room?'

'No. We laid down some traps but none were caught. I believe she then asked the scullery maid for some poison she could put down.'

'You didn't think to mention that to me?'

The housekeeper's shoulders slumped. 'It didn't occur to me to mention it I'm afraid, sir.'

'Right. Never mind.' The detective turned to Mrs Stanley-Piggot again. 'Why did you do it? Why murder three people?'

She said nothing.

Lottie decided to speak up.

'I think it was a mistake,' she said.

'A mistake?' said Mrs Lawrence. 'She murdered three people by mistake?'

'No, two. I think Mrs Stanley-Piggot came here planning murder,' said Lottie. 'But she wasn't successful until the third time.'

'How did you reach this conclusion, Miss Sprigg?' asked the detective.

'I think Mrs Stanley-Piggot intended to murder Daisy Darby. When she heard Miss Darby would be here this weekend, she decided it was her opportunity to strike. I believe that when she murdered Lady Chichester in the maze, she believed she was attacking Miss Darby. I don't know exactly how she prepared for it. Clearly, she was standing on the other side of the hedge with a knife in her hand, listening to their conversation. Perhaps she was trying to peer through as best she could. Perhaps the two women shifted positions at the last moment. But when she jabbed her hand through that hedge, her knife caught Lady Chichester instead of Miss Darby.'

'So my wife was murdered in vain?' said Lord Chichester.

'And my husband?' said Mrs Lawrence.

Lottie nodded. 'As you know, Mrs Lawrence, our cups of tea were in close proximity to each other on that coffee table. Mrs Moore accidentally picked up Mrs Stanley-Piggot's tea at one point. I believe your husband picked up the cup of tea which belonged to Miss Darby.'

Mrs Lawrence glared at Mrs Stanley-Piggot. 'You fiend!' she snarled.

'You finally got Miss Darby in the end,' the detective said to Mrs Stanley-Piggot. 'You entered her room and pushed her off her balcony.'

'Something which I should have done on the first evening,' she said sourly.

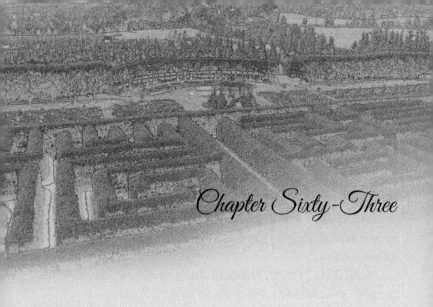

Chapter Sixty-Three

'HERE WE ARE, Lottie, it's all over the morning papers!' said Mrs Moore as she and Lottie breakfasted in her Chelsea home.

Lottie passed a piece of toast to Rosie while Mrs Moore read the newspaper. '"Fake lord exposed" says the headline. It looks like the reporter has done quite a bit of research into the history of Lord Chichester.'

'Does it match what Nellie Harrison told us?'

'Well, she didn't tell us much, did she? She told us just enough to make us suspicious, and you did most of the work, Lottie. And now the newspapers have done the rest.' Mrs Moore read the article, then gave Lottie a summary.

'Lord Chichester's real name is Tommy Brewster. He was born in Camden in north London and his family had very little money. He got involved with some criminals and was arrested for pick-pocketing. After that, he sought his fortune elsewhere, so he stole a bike and rode northwest to the countryside and ended up in Buckinghamshire. It was while he was touring the villages on his bicycle that he came across Lord Chichester in his orchard. He told Lord Chichester he was looking for employment and offered to help him harvest his apples. Lord Chichester took him on, and that was how he found work on the Hamilton Hall estate.

'Lord Chichester was an eccentric character. He never married and had no children. He had inherited a large house and all its land, but he was a troublesome person to get on with. People didn't enjoy working for him. They lasted no longer than a few years. By all accounts, Tommy Brewster was no different. After six months, he had grown tired of the old man's difficult demands. So, that was when he decided to leave, but not before he had hatched a plan.

'Lord Chichester was ninety-five and Tommy Brewster had deduced the old boy wouldn't be around for much longer. He'd also deduced there was no obvious heir to the estate. So he found work on another estate, forged some papers and kept a keen interest in Lord Chichester's health. When Lord Chichester died, he was ready to return to Hamilton Hall. Tommy Brewster introduced himself to everyone as William Chichester, a great nephew of the recently deceased Lord Chichester. He had lots of official-looking paperwork to supposedly prove this, as well as a forged will. He told everyone he'd returned from the Boer War, but there was no evidence he'd ever been involved in it. Before leaving Hamilton Hall, he'd taken a lot of Lord Chichester's personal papers. He claimed that his late great uncle had entrusted him with these papers. As Lord Chichester had not been particularly well-known or well-liked, the family solicitor took him at his word. There was no one else around to contest him. And so, Tommy Brewster became Lord William Chichester.

'Few people in the village questioned his story. They hadn't known the old Lord Chichester well, and the new Lord Chichester was convincing. Most people felt no need to question his story. As the years went by, everybody just assumed he'd always been the natural successor to Hamilton Hall.

'The house had been neglected, but it was filled with

expensive treasures. He set about selling the treasures to fund improvements to the house. He particularly liked the abandoned maze, so he spent some time and money getting it fully restored to its former glory.

'Only one person seemed to realise what he was doing. Her name was Mrs Harrison, and she recalled seeing Tommy Brewster when he was working on Lord Chichester's estate. She tried telling a few people that the new Lord Chichester was not entitled to the estate at all, that he had merely been a worker there for six months. But unfortunately for poor Mrs Harrison, she was dismissed as being mad. Everyone said her spirit had been broken after her husband was killed in the first Boer War. People just dismissed her story as fantasy. She suffered from poor health, and this got the better of her. Before long, she was known as the local madwoman. Dismissed and not listened to. And after all, who would take her word over that of a lord?

'Tommy Brewster, the new lord, married well, and the union with the Forbes family sealed his status. No one could ever possibly question his origin. And as his children were born and grew up in the house, everyone assumed they were a distinguished aristocratic family as reputable as any of the other old families in this country.

'When Nellie Harrison told us about naughty Tommy, I thought she was talking nonsense. I feel quite bad about that now. I suppose we just believed what everyone told us, that she had lost her mind. While there's little doubt that she lost her mind because of the upset of losing her husband in the Boer War, Nellie Harrison wasn't talking nonsense. She realised exactly what had happened, but unfortunately, she lacked the ability to explain it properly to anyone. So for all those years, she talked about naughty Tommy, desperate for some justice to be done. And everybody just dismissed her words as mad ramblings.'

'I wonder what will happen to Tommy Brewster now?' said Lottie.

'Who knows? He's a fraudster, but that's not as bad as being a murderer. And who'd have thought foolish Mrs Stanley-Piggot would have done such a thing? She'd been fooled into buying Nelson's Column and yet she pulled off a murderous feat like that.'

'Perhaps she wanted people to believe she was more stupid than she actually was.'

'Interesting. Perhaps the supposed purchase of Nelson's Column was a ruse to make us think that?'

'I don't know. We'd have to ask her, but we probably wouldn't get a straight answer.'

'There's no telling with some people, is there? Anyway. We have a pile of post to get through here. Oh, there's something for you, Lottie. It's been forwarded on from Fortescue Manor.'

Mrs Moore busied herself with her envelopes while Lottie looked at the little envelope in her hand. Could she cope with being disappointed again?

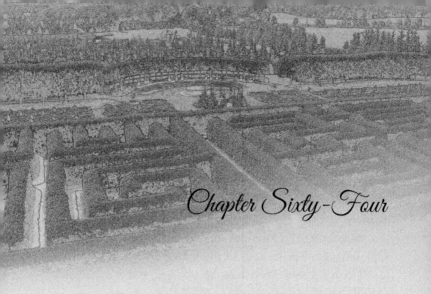

Chapter Sixty-Four

LOTTIE'S HANDS trembled as she opened the little envelope and pulled out the small piece of folded paper.

Dear Miss Sprigg,

Thank you for your letter, I apologise for my late reply. I had to build up my courage before I wrote this.

I am the lady who was asking after you in the orphanage. Please do reply to me once you receive this.

Yours sincerely,

Miss Josephine Holmes

THE END

* * *

Thank you

Thank you for reading this Lottie Sprigg mystery. I really hope you enjoyed it! Here are a few ways to stay in touch:

- Join my mailing list and receive a FREE short story *Murder at the Castle*: marthabond.com/murder-at-the-castle
- Like my brand new Facebook page: facebook.com/marthabondauthor

Murder in the Bay

Book 4 in the Lottie Sprigg Country House Mystery Series

A seaside stay turns sinister!

Lottie Sprigg accompanies her employer on an idyllic break at a coastal country estate. But events take a turn when a body is found in a boathouse. The nearby village of Sherborne-on-Sea has some quirky characters - but is one of them capable of murder?

With the help of her four-legged companion, Rosie, Lottie begins investigating. But someone in the village doesn't want an outsider poking her nose in...

Get your copy: mybook.to/murder-bay

A free Lottie Sprigg mystery

Find out what happens when Lottie, Rosie and Mrs Moore visit Scotland in this free mystery *Murder at the Castle*!

When Lottie Sprigg accompanies her employer to New Year celebrations in a Scottish castle, she's excited about her first ever Hogmanay. The guests are in party spirits and enjoying the pipe band, dancing and whisky.

But the mood turns when a guest is found dead in the billiard room. Who committed the crime? With the local police stuck in the snow, Lottie puts her sleuthing skills to the test. She makes good progress until someone takes drastic action to stop her uncovering the truth...

Visit my website to claim your free copy:

marthabond.com/murder-at-the-castle

Or scan the code on the following page:

Also by Martha Bond

Lottie Sprigg Country House Mystery Series:

Murder in the Library
Murder in the Grotto
Murder in the Maze
Murder in the Bay

Lottie Sprigg Travels Mystery Series:

Murder in Venice
Murder in Paris
Murder in Cairo
Murder in Monaco
Murder in Vienna

Writing as Emily Organ:

Augusta Peel Mystery Series:

Death in Soho

Murder in the Air
The Bloomsbury Murder
The Tower Bridge Murder
Death in Westminster
Murder on the Thames

Penny Green Mystery Series:

Limelight
The Rookery
The Maid's Secret
The Inventor
Curse of the Poppy
The Bermondsey Poisoner
An Unwelcome Guest
Death at the Workhouse
The Gang of St Bride's
Murder in Ratcliffe
The Egyptian Mystery
The Camden Spiritualist

Churchill & Pemberley Mystery Series:

Tragedy at Piddleton Hotel
Murder in Cold Mud
Puzzle in Poppleford Wood
Trouble in the Churchyard
Wheels of Peril
The Poisoned Peer
Fiasco at the Jam Factory
Disaster at the Christmas Dinner
Christmas Calamity at the Vicarage (novella)

Printed in Great Britain
by Amazon